M.

Brick-Dust

Anatiposi

M. M. Pomeroy

Brick-Dust

Reprint of the original, first published in 1871.

1st Edition 2023 | ISBN: 978-3-38212-596-7

Anatiposi Verlag is an imprint of Outlook Verlagsgesellschaft mbH.

Verlag (Publisher): Outlook Verlag GmbH, Zeilweg 44, 60439 Frankfurt, Deutschland
Vertretungsberechtigt (Authorized to represent): E. Roepke, Zeilweg 44, 60439 Frankfurt, Deutschland
Druck (Print): Books on Demand GmbH, In de Tarpen 42, 22848 Norderstedt, Deutschland

BRICK-DUST:

A REMEDY FOR THE BLUES, AND A SOMETHING FOR PEOPLE TO TALK ABOUT.

BY

M. M. POMEROY,

["BRICK POMEROY,"]

AUTHOR OF "SENSE," "NONSENSE," SATURDAY NIGHTS," "GOLD-DUST," ETC.

NEW YORK:

G. W. Carleton & Co., Publishers.

LONDON: S. LOW, SON & CO.

M.DCCC.LXXI.

POPULAR BOOKS

BY

"BRICK POMEROY."

I. —SENSE.

II. —NONSENSE.

III. —SATURDAY NIGHTS.

IV. —GOLD-DUST.

V. —BRICK DUST.

"The versatility of genius exhibited by this author has won for him a world-wide reputation as a facetious and a strong writer. One moment replete with the most touching pathos, and the next full of fun, frolic, and sarcasm."

"I went home with her. She told me all. I could no more. She was a feminine Yankee. She wanted stamps."—*See page* 24.

DEDICATION.

THIS HANDFUL OF

"Brick-Dust,"

GATHERED BY THE WAYSIDE, IS INTENDED AS A *

* * * * * * * * * * * *

* * * * * * * * * * *

* * * * * * * AND TO GIVE

THOSE WHO HAVE NOTHING ELSE TO DO,

SOMETHING TO TALK ABOUT, THAT

THEIR UNFORTUNATE NEIGHBORS

MAY * * * * * *

* * * * * * *

* * * * * *.

THE AUTHOR.

1871.

CONTENTS.

PREFACE.

THIS is the cause of it.

Brick-dust is good to polish—to scour knives, and sharpen things. It is either "light" or "reddy," as the case may be. So will be this book. If you do not like it, do not read it.

If you think you will not like it, do not read it.

If you feel that any of your neighbors will think the less of you for reading the random, ad-cap-tandem ideas, thoughts, surmises, sarcasms, hints, suggestions, conclusions, observations, thinkings, may-bes, or may-not-bes, to be found in the following pages,

> Shun danger, and fly,
> Lest brick-dust in your eye,

or the eye of your neighbor, give you trouble.

Some will like this book.

Some will not.

So of all books—all men—all women—all places—all children.

There is much in the pages of this book people will not understand.

Much others would not have written.

Much we shall never write again!

Just as all of us, in life, at some time, do what we would do over or again.

Some will not like this book because it is personal.

Some will like it for the same reason.

Those who have written better books will pity us.

Those who have written worse ones, we pity!

So, between the two, our "brick" is ground to dust, and somebody will be the gainer.

Any kind of a book is better than talking about your neighbors, when people talk the most about those they know the least of.

For further particulars, inquire within, where will be found pictures of every-day life as they come to

Yours industriously,

"BRICK" POMEROY.

SANCTUM, 1871.

BRICK-DUST.

CHAPTER I.

OUT IN THE GARDEN BOILING SOAP.

THE good old time for boiling soap has come again. The robins tell us so. They know all about the matter; and when they tune up with their playful notes from tree-tops and fence-stakes, then is the time — the golden soap-boiling days — when boys or men drive the stakes and fix the kettle, set the leach-tub, and prepare the kindling-wood.

"Good morning, Mrs. Dinkelson. I told Peter to put our soap-kettle out here near yourn, so 'twould be handy in case of accident. How's yer lye this morning, Mrs. Dinkelson?"

"Oh, purty well. I'm glad you fixed yer kettle over here; it's more sociabeller—at least, it 'pears to me so. How's yer grease?"

"My grease is first-rate—better nor the lye, I 'spect. Did you ever put lime in the bottom of your leach? I told Peter to, but he hadn't got no lime, so he just chucked in some sticks and straw and old rags and a few egg-shells, all smashed up. How much grease you got this spring?"

"Well, I don't 'zactly know, Mrs. Spiker; there is about as much as we allers has—and I don't know as there is, nuther."

"I wish you'd jest ster mine, if I don't get back in time. I must go and tell Jane not to wipe them dishes with the new wipin' cloth; that's for company dishes, and Jane persists in doin' it with that are cloth, just because it's new. I'm mighty 'feared Jane 'll never be like her mother!"

"I'll stir it; but hurry back."

"Well, how was it?"

"Oh, she was usin' it, just as I 'spected. Now I'll stir while you fix the fire. Ain't it nice to have our kettles clus together, so one fire 'll bile both on 'em. It saves wood, and we can get around out of the smoke more easier."

"I allers thought it was a great convenience, 'specially when one has got good neighbors, as we have."

"So do I. Do you put ham-rines in your grease, Mrs. Dinkelson? Peter 'n' I both think it don't come so quick when there's rines in it. Peter's sort of scientific, and 'lows it's the smoke or the saltpetre; but I don't know."

"I allers keeps the rines, Mrs. Spiker. There's so much good grease the other side the rines, it pays to keep 'em. And our folks is such hogs for ham! Mrs. Skypey keeps everything, and she has nice soap, too."

"Well, I don't care for the Skypeys; I knowed

'em when they borrered soap, and never paid it, nuther. She's mighty stuck-up now, since her husband's bought a horse and buggy. It's a good thing everybody ain't proud."

"That's so, Mrs. Spiker. Now, there's Jinkins. He ain't worth more'n my old man, but he makes b'leve he's got more'n ten thousand dollars. An' I can't bear his wife — nasty stuck-up thing, with a boughten petticoat!"

"That *is* so, Mrs. Dinkelson. An' if there *is* any one thing above another that is despisin', it's a boughten petticoat. Better save the money; she'll want it some day."

"Indeed she will. But Mrs. Boggles just knocks Mrs. Jinkins! She's the most extravagantest woman I ever did see. Me and Jedediar has often noticed her doin's. Any woman that's too good to bile soap is just a nasty stuck-up thing; and you know how it is yerself, Mrs. Spiker. I wouldn't miss soap-bilin' for nothin'. It's so sociable to have a real good visit, with nobody to bother us and listen to what we say! And, oh! have you heard of Dekin Jonesby, and what he did to Sally Smiggles?"

"La, me! no. The nasty man! I allers suspected it of him. I never knowed any good of them Jonesbys, and I know it. What did he do?"

"Oh, dear! it's too awful to tell. But I'll just tell *you!* You see, Sally Smiggles went there to do the spring sowin', and one day Mrs. Jonesby was down-town, gaddin' about just as she allers is, when the Dekin cum hum. He let on he didn't know his wife was out; but I know better, and so do you! I jist 'spected what was up, so I run in to borrer a little sal'ratus, all in a hurry, and they was both in the clothes-press! I rushed right in on 'em, but I was a little too soon; they went to fumblin' in the rag-bag. 'Oh!' said I. 'Hello!' said he. 'I just run in for some sal'ratus,' sez I. 'It's in the butt'ry,' said he. 'What yer doin' in here?' sez I.

'Huntin' some linin for Miss Smiggles,' said he. *Huntin' linen!* Yes, I guess it was! An' he looked jest as innercent—the deceivin' wretch! I'm so glad I don't b'long to that church! I'd be afraid of him—the wretch!"

"And Sally Smiggles was in there with him, was she? I allers mistrusted it in her eye!"

"Yes, indeed she was; and she'd her work in her hand, just on purpose to fool me; but I've just been a girl myself, and they can't fool me. I'll tell her mother next Sunday, if I see her."

"Well, the girl cum honestly by it. Her father used to act just so keerless with me, even for a year arter I married Peter. But I knowed him. He used to set on his own door-step every night a whittlin', and when I'd go by he'd look as sweet, and say, 'Good evenin', Mrs. Spiker; won't you call?' and I used to go by every night, just to see if he'd do it!"

"Oh, goodness! it's all runnin' over! Stir it, quick!"

"It's that lime! Skim it!"

"Oh, there goes Dr. Buzley!"

"Goin' down to see Mrs. Spriggers ag'in. It ain't all sickness, and I know it. A man never stays as long with a sick woman as with a well one. He don't stay long when he comes to see me! And he hadn't better. I hate these doctors, who are always makin' examinations of good-lookin' women."

"So do I; and it's good enough for 'em!"

"Have you and Mrs. Brown made up yet?"

"No, we hain't, and I ain't goin' to. It's a pity if our cat can't go over there nights to see their cat, without Brown's shootin' a two-barrelled gun at him! Better keep their cat in the house!"

"That's just what I told Mrs. Rigby."

"What did she say to that?"

"Oh, she acted like a fool, as usual—said 'twas a pity all the cats wa'n't killed. Just because she ain't got no husband, she's awful techy about these things."

"Hello, it's bilin' over ag'in!"

"It's them ar rines — that's what's the matter!"

"Them rines, is it? Then all I've got to say is jest this—Dern the hogs!"

"'*Dern the hogs!*' is it?—'ludin' to me, I 'spose! Then you can jest bile yer own soap, and h'ist yer kittle out'n here to onst!"

CHAPTER II.

THE GOAT. A COMPOSITION ON HIM.

A GOAT is stronger than a pig, and gives milk. He looks at you. So does the doctor; but a goat has four legs. My goat butted Deacon Tillinghast in a bad place, and a little calf wouldn't do so. A boy without a father is an orphan, and if he hain't got no mother he is two orphans. The goat don't give so much milk as a cow, but more than an ox. I saw an ox at a fair one day, and we went in on a family ticket. Mother picks geese in the summer, and the goat eats grass and jumps on a box. Some folks don't like goats, but as for me, give me a mule with a paint-brush tail. The goat is a useful animal, but don't smell as sweet as nice bear's-oil for the hair. If I had too much hair, I would wear a wig, as old Captain Peters does. I will sell my goat for three dollars, and go to the circus to see the elephant, which is larger than five goats.

THOMAS SHINE.

CHAPTER III.

"BRICK" AND HIS PENINNAH!

SHE couldn't help it!

Nor could I!

It rained all day, all night, all the next day, and all the day before—three days! I was walking from plantation to town, near Macon, District of Loyalty. I think it rained, as usual. I saw her gliding from cabin to cabin, from negro house to abode of negro, like a baby duck, much on the waddle. She carried a little cadias in her one hand, and in her other she held high toward the cerulean her skirts, and all sich. She was tall—loveliness on stilts! I saw her from the afterwards—

she had black stockings, wide, blue garters, and moved like a doctor on a visit to his first patient.

I hastened to overtake her. I slid my umbrella over her head. I asked her to excuse me, which she did, and we hitched crooks at once. I was in my element and mud. The woman was white. She was a blushing daughter of New England. She was a gay damsel of many seasons. She was a polisher of Hams. She knew much about Hams. She was a sylph-like educator of niggeroons. She taught education to the ivoryites. She had left the white regions and friends of New England, to come South and tickle the Hams—the little Hams by day and the big Hams by night, as she continued her teaching by light-wood fires in dark woodcabins.

I went home with her. She told me all. I could no more. She was a feminine Yankee. She wanted stamps. Home was nothing; she was on the make. She had not character sufficient to teach school in New England. She was not handsome enough to go to New Orleans by sea, and ride to happiness on an *Evening Star*, so she became a negro schoolist. As a beauty, she was not above par, nor much else. As a scholarist, she was not brilliant. Smoked glass was not needed. As a lover of Hams, she was not severe; but when it came to stamps, she wore her prettys all the time. She told me that her father's name was Stone. Her name was Peninnah—Peninnah Stone. It was a Bible name; it meant *precious* Stone.

Being from home, I was not accountable, so I made love to her, and went with her to school. She moved among the Hams like a silver thimble in a dripping-pan full of breeches-buttons. She wasn't much of a catch, but better than no catch. She was one of the stout-minded. Her early years were spent in chewing gum, weeding onions, pounding stone, and such little amusements, incidental to New England, coupled with psalm-singing and praying for damnation to rest upon all who were sinners.

Peninnah was a sprightly sylph. She could harness an ox, split rails, stick a hog, and do all manner of such music.

We loved. It was a matter of profit. Being a New Englander, she had no heart. Simply a Stone. Harder than a Brick. We walked about among the cabins of her lambs. She was chief engineer of a nigger-teaching shop, and boss of a mammoth carpet-bag. We meandered under the black-jacks and honeysuckles. First she'd sling her arms about my neck and kiss me, then she'd kiss the little lambs—dear little Hams! Said I:

"Peninnah, sweet one, why kissest thou the little he-thopians?"

Then she bent her eyes into me, and said:

"The more we kiss 'em, the more hair-oil, brass rings, photographs, and playthings we sell 'em!"

Ah, I see, charming Peninnah! Kiss 'em—kiss 'em all around, from cabin to cabin, from

Ham to Ham, from infancy to old age, and sell 'em gewgaws—for of such is the kingdom of New England, and he-thopians are the profit.

And we sat on a mossy bank, watching the little Hams basking in the sun as they wallowed in the warmth, and thus braided our love together. Said my sweet Peninnah:

"Oh, Brick, it's nice! Let us wed and be happy. I'll support you. I'm a Yankee schoolist, not handsome enough to be ornamental, or I'd gone farther South. But I'm several on the make. I'll make mutton of these lambs, in time. There is no need of us at home, so I came here to make money. I kiss the little Hams; I pets 'em and I caress 'em; I tell 'em that the good Abrum was their saviour; that he sent me here on purpose; that I love 'em so dearly; that they are—oh! *so sweet* to me, and that, in a few years, each of 'em, male and female, shall be in Congress from Massachusetts. And I pats their little heads, and I kiss their little lips, and I sell 'em primers and readers at five hundred per cent. profit, and I sell 'em 'purty things,' and I fines 'ém for not learning their lessons, and I sells each of 'em my photograph for a dollar, and I sells each of 'em *blue clay greased* for half a dollar a box, and I manage to hoax the little Hams out of all their stamps, and to make teachin' a big business. Ain't I a nice girl, dear, dear, gentle Brick?"

And she kissed me again and again, till I had a link of wool left on my lips, when with a smile she pillowed my agile head on her spiral indicators, and went on:

"Oh, it's nice to be a he-thopian schoolist! We are from home. We are on the make. There are some teachers here who are good, but not sharp. They don't speculate, as we do; they simply teach for their salaries. But they are not full Yankees—only half-breeds. I can make enough here in a year, off and on, to buy a plantation; then we'll set up for nabobs! Let us wed! I'll teach 'em; you soap 'em. We'll wed. You go North as a Southern loyalist; I'll go North as an injured female. We'll do the darkeys, then do the soft ones in the North. This is a big business. I'm from New England—on the make. Let's unite, and be happy!"

I'm to wed Peninnah. She is a most desirable darling. So sweet, so kind, so financial in her affections, such a devoted Christian, that I know we shall be happy. And we'll be rich. While I whine injured loyalty up North, Peninnah will skin the Hams here. We'll soon be bond-holders, exempt from taxation, and regular New England aristocrats. Bring me a little nigger—sweet little Ham; let us kiss him once for Peninnah!

CHAPTER IV.

CAT LYRICS.

CONFOUND the yowling cats!
Why don't they hunt for rats?
Or keep as still as bats
Or moles, out on the flats?
At dead of night
They yowl and fight—
Till one would think they were a match
For the father of cats—the old scratch
They steal all our cream!
They burst on our dream,
As with spitter and sputter
With yowl and with mutter—
As out by the gate
One stops with his mate
To give us the devil—a cat serenade!
To waken us up when in bed we are laid.

What are they fit for, the noisy things?
How we wish they were drown-ded
Or into jell pounded—
Or all of them turned into new fiddle-strings!
For the mice and the rats,
And some neighbor's brats
And the bricks in our hats
And the child scaring bats
Are not half the bother of night-yowling cats!
As with sca-t-t-tr-r and y-e-*ow!*
They cause us to vow
If we get out of bed
Each cat will be dead
That has mounted the shed
And forced us to swear
At all the cats there!
But when the lamp it is lit and we start with a gun
We can't catch the devils, no matter if we run!

You may sing little ditties
To cats and their kitties —
May possibly be able with cats to agree:
But we prefer rats
To the best of your cats,
Be it a pet cat — a he or a she.
Their holes you can fill
The rats you can kill —
Bury all in a heap
Then quietly sleep,

But the devil's companions in numerous numbers
Have so often and oft woke us from our slumbers,
  That we prefer brats,
  Muskeeters or rats,
To your treacherous, yowling, sputtering cats,
That ought to be plunged in hot-water vats!

CHAPTER V.

RIDING A VELOCIPEDE.

OF course we have been on it. Show us any infernal machine constructed through the ingenuity of man for the breaking of bones, ripping open of cuticle, damage of eyes, warping of backbones, perpetrating of contusions on head, or anything of that sort, that we have not been on or dare not try. Velocipede is a good thing, if you don't have too much of it; and you can't have too much of it unless you get more than you want. Everybody rides velocipedes nowadays. The ladies ride them. The men ride them. The boys ride them. Men ride them for fun and ride them in earnest. And the confoundedest, stand-up-fall-down-ingest thing a man, woman, or child ever saw, is a velocipede.

They are erected on two wheels; one wheel being immediately in front of the other wheel, and the other wheel being immediately behind t'other wheel. This makes it more binding on the part of the operator. There are no axle-trees, no yard-arms, bolster, lobster, or other paraphernalia pertaining to ox-carts, wagons, bob-sleds, railroad cars, steamboats, balloons, or any other inventions for locomotion yet discovered. There is a little thing runs through one wheel on which it revolves. It comes straight up like the national tax, then slants back four perches, five links, and six degrees; then jabs downward to the little thing in the hind wheel, and thus ends the first chapter, and likewise the next. At the front end, when it is not going backward, there is a contrivance resembling an auger, by which the ambitious goest turns, returns, upturns, overturns, and turns out of the way. Because of the auger in front, no one should consider the velocipede a perfect bore. Instead, it is a perfect goer; for many a man, in learning to go on it, has started his gore in more places than lightning ever struck a one-eyed pilot. The concern has a spine, or backbone, which is used as a roof for the two wheels. The wheels are three-quarters of an inch wide. The backbone, or roof, is an inch and a quarter wide. On this backbone is affixed a cast-iron pad resembling in shape the frontispiece of some Dutch target company's parade-cap, except that the points of the pad are so arranged as to hurt you while mounted on this aforesaid invention of agony. As a horsebackist, we have been called a success. Once we rode a mule. On another occasion we rode a brindle cow home from the fair — not to add to our comfort, but to pay the aforesaid bovine for not drawing the premium. On another occasion we undertook to ride a speckled steer, but for some reason or other his finis department had a sudden inclination to elevate itself into the air, and we dismounted over his head, simply because the mane of the beast did not amount to much for hanging-on purposes. On another occasion we rode a saw-mill saw for half an hour, but we never tried it again.

But we did try the velocipede. We got astride of it and started. Immediately after, a gentleman was discovered lying on the ground, to the merriment of lookers-on. Once more we mounted the breach, if by these words a cast-iron pad may be called, and undertook to propel the invention. Just then a gentleman struck his head with extreme violence against the curb-stone. More merriment. Another attempt, and just then a gentleman was discovered sprawling upon the ground, with his left ear full of mud. More merriment, but not on the part of the victim. Again we got well under way, by the aid of two men to push and a small boy to steer, while we

"If there's some fellow you have a spite against, coax him to try a velocipede."—*See page* 39.

were getting used to the contrivance; but at such an hour as we knew not, our assistants departed from us. We made two lunges ahead, and, while endeavoring to turn out for a young lady, cramped the wrong way, collided, took her on the invention in front of us, and we both went off together, to the damage of a $10 hat and a $23 Grecian bend. The glory of that hat and that bend departed with much quickness, never more to return. As for the lady, we pray the Lord to pardon her for the feelings she entertains toward us, for really we could not help it!

Well, we tried it again. Undertook to cross the street, and accidentally ran plumb against the hind end of a charcoal wagon. We got off, while the industrious velocipede took a scoot to the left, landing in the gutter. Such a nice place to put your feet! Good deal like sitting on a grindstone, turning it with your toes. Aside from the delightful sensation experienced, it strains the muscle, and is more wearing upon garments.

Riding a two-story Indiana hog just turned loose to fat on beach-nuts, would be sweet cream in comparison with this invention. Sliding down-hill on a hand-saw tooth-side up, would be two degrees more comfortable than experimenting on one of these contrivances; but then, it is fashionable! If any of our readers have a suit of clothes they wish to spoil, seven or eight pair of legs they would lame for seven weeks, a high-finished and moral back they don't care for, fifteen or sixteen yards of court-plaster, a dozen or more new hats, several pairs of boots, and the Lord only knows how many coat-tails to spoil, let them buy a velocipede, and commence practice at once. To purchase one of the confounded things requires but a small fortune—say twice as much as is necessary to purchase a hand-cart, which is by far the most comfortable to ride on; while a few dollars extra would last about four hours for insurance against accidents. Go and try it. Buy one. But first, employ a physician by the month, to doctor you for all bruises, contusions, sprains, rheumatism, compound vulgar and improper fractions, and every ailment under the sun, when you may be happy yet. We have tried it. The next day the velocipede went off as smoothly as usual, but as to its rider, that's altogether another matter. We have not been able to walk up and down stairs without the aid of a cane for a week —have hardly spoken a good-natured word for a fortnight. Our best pants are at the tailor's; and not less than ninety-three bottles of liniment stand grinning at us from every room we occupy during the day. If there is some fellow you have a spite against, coax him to try a velocipede; when, in all probabilities, he will bring an action against you for wilful intent to murder, or, at least, assault and battery—and make his action stick.

CHAPTER VI.

SAILORS' DANCE-HOUSE.

IF a man has the blues and is dissatisfied with life, let him come with us to-night and to-morrow night, then let him go with us the next day afternoon on a visit to the poor of New York. Out on God's green fields, surrounded with the free air and growing vegetation, beneath the crimson sunsets of the West, we know not what it is to *half live*, or how our fellows do. And 'tis well we do not from experience.

Down on Water street, in the great city of New York, and on other streets also, are to be found sailors' boarding-houses, sailors' homes, sailors' clothing-stores, and sailors' dancing-rooms. The latter we have visited, and there learned a lesson.

At twelve o'clock we passed along the street, east from the Battery. Over the open door of a two-story wooden building hung a glass gas-lamp, on which was painted an anchor and two dancing-girls. Passing in at the door, we were in a small bar-room, the floor neatly sanded, a few lithographs on the walls, a few chairs standing around, a round table on which was a backgammon-board and some well-fumbled newspapers; some tissue-paper cut in fancy shapes and patterns ornamented the ceiling; a screen, or stationary blind, stood in one corner of the room; a bar well filled with nicely-polished, partly-filled glass decanters, presided over by a hawk-eyed man, and, with the exception of two strangers sipping a claret punch, the room is inventoried.

Bowing to the bar-tender, who winks in return, we pass behind the screen, open a still-shutting door, and the bright gas-light shows the way down a flight of stairs. At the top of the stairs, inside the door, sits a man who takes from you two shillings, and in return gives back a dirty card. At the foot of the stairs you find another man, who takes the card and admits you into a room, in which, if you choose, you may safely leave your hat or coat, receiving therefor a check till you see fit to return. Then through a side-door, down a second flight of stairs, and into a well-lighted but not well-ventilated room about fifty feet by seventy.

This is the place; let us look around a wee bit.

At the right is a bar extending clear across the room. In front is a narrow but high stage, on which are five musicians. Hard seats are ranged around all sides of the room, on which are sitting men, principally sailors, eager for fun, and women who could gain admittance here without exhibiting a marriage certificate. There are one or two black women and a few black men, but they do not seem to confine their attention to those of their own color.

Fashion had little to do with dress here — tawdry finery, draggled silk dresses full short above, gay tinselled head-dresses, cheap jewelry, and paint. Wrecks of humanity! Forms once loved, oh, how well! Hopes once so bright, now turned to ashes. God pity them! Here they can drown their sorrow, and nightly reach another mile-stone on the road to hell. In they came till the room was full, and soon the dancing began. No one waited for an introduction, but each one sailed in on his own hook, dancing and drinking, joking and laughing.

The room was close and hot. Two stories under ground, it could not well be otherwise, when a hundred half-intoxicated men and women, both black and white, were singing and dancing and sweating down there like crazy devils. The plain but heavy oak bar across the far end of the room was covered with slops and thick, heavy glasses, which would serve as slung-shots for a week without being broken or cracked. By one o'clock the fun was lively. The space in front of the bar was crowded, and a constant stream of "blue ruin" went sizzling down the throats of the sailors and their partners. The six bar-tenders, with short hair, round heads, thick, short lips, red shirts, and arms bared, sweat like a man cradling, as they flew around from bottle to bottle, making change for this party, swearing at that one, and ordering back those who had just drank.

The music struck up for a waltz. A tall, corpulent sailor, who would weigh at least two hundred and thirty pounds, with a half-drunken woman nearly his equal in size, jumped for the lead, and away they went—around and around! In twenty seconds fifty couple were whirling and twirling, till it seemed to us as if the room was a large churn, and the inmates were so many sticks rattling and jolting together as it went flying around. Hot! A hay-field was nothing to it. Away they went circling around, black and white; here a big black fellow hugging a once beautiful white girl in close embrace; there a red-nosed American, two-thirds drunk, with the head of a black, greasy-looking wench lovingly reclining on his shoulder, his coarse, *meaty* hand half-imbedded in the thick fat of her sides; yonder a short-legged German and a slim-waisted girl whirling like a top, till it made one dizzy to look at them.

In five minutes all were tired out, and had marched to the bar, except the big couple and the American with the fat wench. Around the large room they went, keeping step to the music. Others turned to watch them, when one fellow with a sailor-jacket on sang out:

"Heave ahead, old merchantman!"

And he did "heave ahead," the little chap close behind.

"I'll go the grog on the *slaver!*" sang out a

jolly-looking chap who was fanning himself with his tarpaulin.

"Ole V'ginny neber tiah!" lisped the wench, as she passed the corner where our party stood, her black, greasy face looking with Ethiopian fondness into the face of her partner, and her musk-ular bosom heaving and tossing like a bum-boat at anchor in a storm!

"*C-o-m-e i-n!*" sang out old corpulence, as he whirled past, panting for breath.

The crowd was excited, and even forgot to drink, so anxious were they to see who would tire out first; and their remarks were in earnest, if not fashionably expressed:

"Heave up, my hearty!"

"Go in, little 'uns—a black sky and a white!"

"Two to one on the whales!"

"That's a go for the grog!"

"*Rip!* my sweet Creole! If you beats 'Top-light Bill,' I wants a piece of you!"

On they went, panting, sweating, and waltzing, with "Toplight Bill" and the "Creole" ahead.

The big couple were good dancers, but in a strife of this kind the lighter couple had the advantage, and in ten minutes from the time the trial began, "Toplight Bill" and his sunburnt partner had the floor! Twice around the room they went, after the other couple had given out, then marched to the bar, blowing and puffing like a horse with the heaves.

Drinking over for a few moments, and while the crowd were waiting for the music to wet up.

"Give us a song, Shorty!" sang out a very free-and-easy sailor, who evidently did not care whether school kept or not.

"A song—a song—a song—yes, a song—a jolly good 'un!" sang out a score of voices, when a fancy-looking little fellow, about five feet no inches, in sailor-dress, stepped out on the floor, and in a fine alto voice began:

Jack's alive and merry, boys,
  When he's got the rhiners;
Heh! for rattle fun and noise,
  Hang all grumbling whiners.
Then drink, and call for what you please,
  Until you've had your whack, boys;
We think no more of raging seas,
  Now we have come back, boys.

Chorus, in which about twenty voices joined, keeping time by slapping their hands on their legs:

Rip, Skip! spoodledy whang,
Skip galore, scatter a wee;
Rip Skip! jig it again
Grog galore and off to sea!

"Bravo! bravo!"

"Don't stop, little one," as the singer was about to step back.

Jack's alive, and full of fun;
  At sea or shore he's jolly,
With a helping hand for every one
  And a sailor's heart for Polly.
Then drink, and call for what you please,
  Until you've had your whack, boys;
We think no more of raging seas
  For Polly has brought us back, boys!

Chorus, &c.

"Partners for a hornpipe!" rang out a square-shouldered, muscular man, the "boss" of the concern. He was dressed in style, with check pants, square-toed boots for kicking, red under and white over shirt, both unbuttoned at the collar, sleeves rolled up, and hat removed from a close-cropped head. He was about five feet eight inches high, square frame, looking like a tough nut to crack, as he was. His eye was all over the room, and we noticed that, whenever he went up to a noisy fellow and told him kindly to "go slow," the noisy individual thought it good advice, and gave heed.

We never saw the sailors' hornpipe *danced* till we saw it here, and the exhibition of agility was worth a day's journey. One might as well try to keep track of a flea by moonlight, as to try to tell whose bodies the hundred legs on the floor belonged to. This dance over, another rush to the bar, another hoisting in of bottled death, and another song by a black-whiskered boatswain's mate:

> Steer clear from the musty old lubbers
> Who tell us to fast and to think,
> And patient fall in with life's rubbers
> With nothing but *water to drink!*"

Chorus, as before, but sung in a slow strain:

> But water?
> Cold water!
> Fresh water!
> Weak water!
> Thin water!
> With nothing — but water — to drink!

"Come on, my hearties! let's splice the main again; then for the Barbadoes jig!"

While the crowd was surging up toward the bar, we stood and carefully scanned the motley assemblage. Most of them were from twenty-one to middle age, although among the men were a few old salts whose hair was turning gray. Most of them were sailors, intent on fun and spending their hard-earned money; and, what between poor whiskey and other pleasures, they were in a fair way to soon be ready for another cruise. With a few exceptions, there was nothing ugly about the countenances of the motley crowd assembled there. Good nature, carelessness, love of fun, and a sort of jolly independence, were the chief traits discernible. They—the sailors—had long been absent from shore-scenes and pleasures, and were evidently bound to have a good time; and their partners, who frequent such places, and literally "freeze" to the poor tar soon as he returns from a cruise, till his money be spent, were as attentive and loving as a poor sailor could wish.

Here, in this and kindred saloons, night after night, commencing about midnight, does the fun—song and dance—have full sway. Here is the sailor robbed, and, with empty purse and disease renewed, soon fitted for another voyage! When the song is loudest, the passer-by on the street would not dream that under his feet was so much noise, or that, in through that nicely-sanded bar-room, behind that green shade, was a door leading down two flights of stairs—so far down that the horn of Gabriel would fail to arouse passers-by; yet such is the case.

The keepers of these places make money, and not a few of them are owned by up-town merchants, who employ a trusty man as overseer. The small admittance-fee of twenty-five cents more than pays the music and rent; while the profits from the sale of doctored liquors and vile cigars cannot be short of a hundred dollars a night.

CHAPTER VII.

A War Tale.

CHAPTER THE ONE.

IT was night—the hub of it!

CHAPTER THE SECOND.

"And now, daughter, go to your retiracy! Muchly as I love you, and zephyr-like as your frail body is to me, I tell you, nymph, thou shalt never marry Theophilus. He is poor. You are rich. The noble house of Squiggers shall never be dishonored by menial blood."

CHAPTER TWO-AND-ONE.

"Theophilus Honeybalm, go hence! How dare you, a hired man in the employ of your Mehitable's father, look upon my child to woo? Begone! You have no position. My nymph-like child shall never wed and bear children to any man who is not noble."

CHAPTER THE AND-SO-FOURTH.

"Come to the window, child!" It was June. "Why art so cast down, wasted beauty?" She had grown thin of meat. "I will find for thee a mate, sweet bird of song!" Mehitable sang a little while washing dishes.

"What ho, without!" Somebody was knocking on the door.

CHAPTER FIVE.

"H-a-a-a-a-a-lt!" spake in gentle tones the intruder. It was General Theophilus Honeybalm!

"Tis h-e-e-e-e-e-e!" That's what Mehitable gave utterance to.

"Yes, 'tis he! I come! Stand back, old man! To the rear! Ten paces backward MARCH!"

Old Squiggers retrograded, 'cause Theophilus had a whang-striker in both hands, red with—rust.

"Now, old man"—so said the General—"I come to claim my bride; I am a B. G.—a Brig.-Gen. Three long months have flewded. I am now a great man. Seest thou this pile of gold? I have a million! I have houses and lands. I have position. I have honor. I wrote a puff for my General! I was given a nigger regiment. For fifty dollars' worth of mules I bribed the telegraph to record my daring deeds. I came out for the brunette part of this Government! The President rewarded me. I am a General of Ethiopianos!"

Then whispered the sire:

"General, are you honest?"

"Are I honest? Do the world exist? I are. It do! Else I were not a General."

"Then take her. I am satisfied. The country is safe. My child, be happy!"

And he took her.

This ends a history of love and loyalty.

CHAPTER VIII.

RACE ON THE PRAIRIE.

ELEVEN o'clock!

Sharp to the second struck the bell.

"All aboard!" shouted the conductor, as we reached up for the iron hand-help and sprang to the floor of Engine No. 199, just starting from Chicago eastward for New York.

A more beautiful, life-giving morning we never knew. Saturday morning in that great city of the West—that eighth wonder of the world! An appointment made by telegraph, to be at our office at sharp seven o'clock Sunday evening. We were in a hurry—like a pendulum vibrating between important interests, marking time and events for others. So we asked for the quickest route; and a good friend gave proof that his route over the Alleghany Mountains was the quickest, easiest, and the best. And so we hastened to the depot, quickly as whirling carriage-wheels and fast horses could take us, just in time for the bell—and the

"*All aboard!*"

Ever by choice at the front—out of the dust and into the danger; for, in case of a collision, it would be glorious to rush into eternity and tell them:

"The rest of the mangled delegation will be here in a minute!"

Riding on the engine! How clear and bright! Everything in perfect order. The polished steel, iron, and brass mirrored faces, forms, and scenery. The sharp-eyed, cool-brained, steady-nerved, temperate engineer, knows his business, from the lightest puff of steam to the handling of that mighty mass of machinery, as a mother would the babe dandled on her knees.

The fireman rang the engine-bell, and fed the glowing mouth of the tamed fiend we were on. Out from Chicago—slowly, steadily out from the cross-streets, store-houses, homes of workers, crossing lines of railroads, huge granaries and mammoth elevators, where wheat is lifted and stored for market.

Out from the wide-spreading, wonderful city—past little houses and big ones—past the grimy-looking men with little signal-flags at road-crossings—past the halted processions of drays, carts, wagons, milk pogies, carriages, and business life; out into the broad, beautiful prairie country, where God's mighty thunder has rolled all inequalities of elevation to a level!

Out from the city at last. Out from municipal regulation as to speed of train. At liberty now to begin our journey as the storm-clouds travel.

The fireman lets loose from the bell-rope, swings open the furnace-door, and with wood tickles the palate of the devil's baby we are riding on, till it inner-whistles, chuckles with delight, throws out its mesmerism of power, trembles with created emotion, and seems ready to leave the smooth, silver-topped steel rails, and fly through the air.

But the little man with eye like that of an eagle—with skull-cap drawn tight over his head—with look close upon and far-reaching the rails before him—with mind intent only on his duties and responsibilities, rests his hand on that little steel pulse-bar; the powerful pet he so masters by a touch loses its nervousness, as does a woman when the strong arm of a fearless man is thrown between her and danger.

Faster—faster—*faster*—*faster!*

Out and away! Twenty, twenty-five, thirty miles an hour. Only playing with distance as yet! We are only picking up the mile-posts slowly now, looking at them and throwing them down!

Ha, ha!

A rival on the road! Once more at your old tricks! Right ahead of us, as the arrow flies to its rest, runs our line of track, miles away. And to our left, not more than a pistol-shot distant, is another track, and, like the one we are on, straight ahead for miles, till, following the marking of the builders, the road bears away to the left and the northward.

And on that track, out from Chicago, comes a light, rakish-looking train—the lightning-express; four long, light passenger-cars. But *there* is grace of motion for you! The cloud of black smoke miscegenating with the white steam lifts itself up into air for the rushing train to pass under. The red driving-wheels of the beautiful engine reach into the distance with their connecting-bar arm, short, quick, snappish, and the train rushes by. The engineer over there nods at us from his cab-window; the fireman looks at us with gyrating thumb to his nose; the brakemen on that flying train shake hands at us, as if to say, "Good-bye; if you are in a hurry, send along with us;" the passengers at the windows wave their handkerchiefs, and motion for us to "come on!"

Really, that is very nice—when we are in haste, and those on that train are travelling East, as we are! And, in less time than we have consumed in writing the two preceding paragraphs, the rival train is half a mile ahead of us, flying like a devil-kite over the flat-land.

Smile? Not a bit. We looked at the engineer, who seemed to know his business! He looked at us once; there was a nod—it was enough. Then he looked at our young friend, master of transportation, with us on the engine. Another answering nod.

Business, now! The fireman jerked open the furnace-door, and into the livid throat of our devil-pet went the wooden lunch, to be fire-gravied and devoured. The engineer pulled that skull-cap a little closer over his eyes, and opened the window before him; then his left foot reached down to the brace, as if to say something to the network of mechanism! Then he leaned forward just a little, like a jockey winning the Derby, took hold of the lever, and pulled so slowly and firmly that it seemed as if he was in love with his engine.

Thank you! A little more steam—and the engine whistled its thanks and laughed in a tremor of delight! Another slow pull on that lever-bar, a steady hand held there, and see how beautifully our prairie-chaser settles to the work!

Faster!

Faster!

FASTER!

Thirty-five miles an hour!—forty miles an hour!—forty-five miles an hour!—fifty miles an hour! And still faster! We are after that rakish-running fugitive ahead of us on that other track! And that train is flying wild! The mile-posts fairly dance, to be thrown, as it were, without a notice, a mile to our rear! The engine has no time to tremble now; there is work being done! It seems as if we were fairly flattening to the track—hugging the earth—rushing like a storm-courier into eternity! The engineer looks not from the rail; his hand comes not from the bar—and *still faster* we rush on, as never before.

Did you ever see a juggler swallow a sword? So are we swallowing the line of open space between the trains! Like two scared devils are these two engines working their best. That one over there is a beauty; but this one is "old business!" We come up to the rear end of the train; the brakeman on the rear platform, as we are opposite him with the engine, turns away in disgust. Now for it, red-hot! Just a little more steam, and we shoot by like a dart, as if it was *so easy!* The passengers on that train wave no more handkerchiefs; there is a long white flash of them from the windows of our cars, as we look back.

We quietly motion to the engineer over there to try it again. He shakes his head, and thinks —as did the Dutchman's boy!

Here we are—they are there! And then, as speed was slackened, our engineer says, with a smile:

"*Good morning!*"

And the two trains went on their way as if nothing had happened—as there had not—only a race—a going a little faster than usual rate of speed, out of compliment to a perfect track and the perfection of machinery.

"A good engine!"

"You are right—the best in the world."

"Where was she made?"

"At our shops."

"A model piece of work."

"Yes, sir; our boys know their business."

And the engineer looked so lovingly and approvingly on the beauty on which we rode—the strength, the polish, the perfection of ingenuity. The fireman opened the door so we could hear the little devils in the hot throat and livid furnace laugh and chuckle over the work so well done under the guiding hand of a brave man, who could tame the elements to annihilate space.

* * * * * *

And we looked at the country—at the beautiful engine—at the long stretch of railroad—at the *work* men had done for such great purpose.

Then we sat on the cushioned seat so kindly given up to us by the fireman, who soon will be an engineer, and thought of the earnest workers of the land—of the braw-armed mechanics, whose muscle we almost envy—of their clink-clank on anvils—of their work over hot fires—of their daily, daily, daily work—of their wives and their little ones—of their sweethearts and their hopes for the future—of the earnest life they are living—of the work they are doing for the benefit of our country.

And we thought of the men on farms, the women in farm-houses, the children who wish for better homes, better education, better clothing, and how proud we were to know that these working-men, working-women, and working-children were, and are, entitled to the honor of making our country great.

Then, we thought, as the train flew on, as the engineer managed the beautiful machinery made by other workingmen, as the fireman threw in the wood cut by other workingmen, as we rode over the roads laid by still other workingmen, as we dashed by the homes of yet other working-men, as we hastened on to help our *workingmen*, how glorious it is to live and be of some use in this world, which is one of the little machine-shops of the universe.

And we said, while thinking of what the sawers of wood, the drawers of water, the miners of metals, the pounders of iron, the cookers of food, the workers everywhere are doing to help themselves, and help each other:

God love the workers of America, and *damn the Power that will not protect them!*

CHAPTER IX.

REMINISCENCE OF ROXELIA.

YOU never saw Roxelia Powlowker, the crimson-haired daughter of General Washington Powlowker, of Boston, did you? If not, I'll tell you about her. She is married, now—has been for years. But she was not then.

I was a boy—a pale-eyed songling of some note, but not possessed of much wealth. My parents were honest people. General Powlowker lived in a stone house—a large edifice, with not less than nineteen rooms inside, and room for more outside. Mrs. Powlowker called it a *stun* house; but she was always so facetious.

Mrs. Powlowker was General Powlowker's wife—lawfully wedded unto him a long time previous. His father was one of them as fit into the Revolution. He, too, had a contract—took his pay in Continental money, bought land, loaned it out in corner-lots with mortgage security, and took on style. He must have been possessed of at least several thousand dollars, if not more. He was a respectable man. He never drank out of a bottle. He never swore before the preacher, or other company. But sometimes, in the barn, or when a wasp would sting into him he would converse in dialect most sulphurious.

He had five children—three boys, and two who were pretty near boys. Roxelia was one of the latter.

I was one of the boys she used to be pretty near, only when the old gent would catch us at it! Then he objected. Once or twice he objected with a boot. But did true love *ever* run smooth?

I heart-hankered for Roxelia. She was fair to look upon. She had health—about one hundred and eighty pounds of it. And her face! It was all there. And her feet! What sighs!—as I think of those. And her hair! Like her heart—to love her Markuel, decidedly ready.

She was to have property some day. We all desire property. As a nation of accumulators, we are a general success. I was not rich, but was willing to be. And I did love Roxelia. She was the first girl I ever saw so much of. There was not so much of any other girl as of her.

How I courted that girl! The first eggs of spring I found in her father's barnary and laid in her lap. The early birch-bark and the pristine juvenile wintergreen, with an occasional slip of prince's pine, would I besiege her with. The language of the latter—I pine for thee, O Roxelia.

I desired to become wedlockically acquainted

with her. I visited her Saturday nights, and stayed till Morpheusly sleepy. But not when the old man was there. I looked with luscious eye on the time when I could be son-in-law to the General. But I was poor. My home was in a blacksmith-shop—part of the time. Because I at times was caught at a vise, the old man had no use for me. He asked if I had money.

"No, no, old man," I said.

But Roxelia did not detest me. Oft have I sat on the fence and looked in at her window. Often did I stand and see her father walk by. But he never noticed me. But I did his girl. We planned elopements. We sat, and sighed, and squeezed each other's hands. It is justly supposed to be fun. Indeed it is. So we liked it. Roxelia liked it, too. We made affection to each other. We met by moonlight. Once she moved forth from her chamber-window and sat on the wood-shed roof. I would shed my blood as that wood-shed roof would shed rain; and so, anxious lad that I was, I laddered myself up to her side, and reposed with my head in her lap, till each of us took a cold in the head. But what is cold in the head to a heart all aflame with a consuming fire? Colds troubled Roxelia. They were red-headitary in the family. But she went not into the chamber that night, like a turtle in his palace, till we had plighted. When should come the spring-time, we were to wed. This contract was negotiated in the gentle autumn, when the moon was in its mooniest glory, and chickens had not read of Thanksgiving terrors.

Then I was very happy. I slid off that roof as easy! Who cares for ladders, when happiness fills him like smoke in a new church? What if a brave boy sprains his knee and destroys the wholeness of wearing apparel, if his Roxelia has only anchored her head on his shoulder, and said yea to his enticements?

The next day I went to work with renewed cheerfulness. It was of the vernal time coming, and of Roxelia, that I thought, and of our coming joys, and home, and hen-coops, and good clothes, and 'lasses, and looking-glasses, and perhaps of other responsibilities, when I should earn them.

The next night, like a dutiful girl, she told her paternal that she had chosen and had promised to wed with the object of her father's cholorousness. He was angry—perhaps more. He took hold of her ear with vehemence. He wafted her from him. He said she was no daughter of his—which was a rough joke on her mother, to say the least. But the General was angry. He threatened convent for the girl and double-barrelled shot-gun for the boy. But she was firmness. Then I loved Roxelia none the less. Quite to the very contrary.

So we sat in meditation and apprehension.

And alas!

One day a man came there, who was a scion of wealth, who boasted of pedigree, who wore oil on his mustache, who carried a cane, and wore cream-colored kids. He spake French, and Greek, and Russian, and other oddities, to me. He was the Count Somebody. He talked with the General. He played sweet on the fair Roxelia. He minced his language He boasted of his paternity, and of his beautiful home by the sea. As a talker, he was a success.

Good-by, boy in a blacksmith-shop!

When the vernal season came, there was a wedding. The Count and Roxelia were the ones. She turned up her nose at me. Old Powlowker wanted me to come and black boots for the Count the night he was to be married. He said it was an honor he would confer upon me. I went—not much!

Time has been flying a few years.

I saw Roxelia to-day. Her Count was also a banker—a large dealer. But he dealt fair-O! he did. Old Powlowker thought he was a catch. So did Roxelia. So it was—for Roxelia. Now she has two or three little Counts. She tends an oyster saloon in the Bowery. I have been there twice to-day—once for a stew, once for a few raw. She does not know me now. Her husband holds a position in Sing-Sing—three years yet to serve.

To-morrow I will drive by her saloon, and perhaps step in and order a broil, or a dozen on the half-shell. She seems to understand the business. Maybe I will ask her if she ever lived at ———, and knew old General Powlowker, or if she remembers him? I will tell her my name is Norval, or Jones, or Perigrew, or Winterset, or something. Her father is older now. So is Roxelia. He was quite rich then. But that was before the war—before his daughter married a Count, and before the boy who worked in a blacksmith-shop, and had no fine shirt to wear, was

Rememberingly thine.

CHAPTER X.

KU-KLUX!

TO THE PRESIDENT OF THE UNITED STATES: to the Senate and House of Reprobates, and all other loyal citizens at home or roaming:

This, the prayer of your outraged petitioner, prayeth—Selah!

My name, which it is Wandering V. A. Bond. My father made basswood hams, and that was the cause of it. The amateur part of my variegated life was spent in New Hampshire. Educated on two catechisms — one Kittychism and baked beans on Sunday, I skinned cats on Monday for worrying rats on the Sabbath, and thus became one of the anointed. Ours was a Christian neighborhood. The song of praise in the morn, and the flipping of coppers for the contents of the contribution-plate, were heard each Sabbath, while the sisters of the flock poured molasses and the rum of New England together for evening devotions and ornamenting of puritanical noses.

This, by way of prelude.

When the war came I was at home, busy at my avocation. I heard the harsh tocsin of fight. It wakened me from my afternoon nap on a bench in the corner grocery, and kindled a new impulse into me. It filled me with martial desire. I sold my clam-cart, and laid my all on the altar of Government. I was commissioned by the best President of the best Government the best people in the best world ever saw, to arm and go forth as a Chaplain, to fight the enemies of Gog and Magog, Shadrach, Abraham, and Belial.

In two days I fitted myself for the ministry; in one day fitted for war — a cerulean uniform and an empty trunk. At the expense of our good Government I rode forth by sea and by land, on foot and on horseback; going up and down the earth, preaching currant-jelly for the stomach, plunder for the body, and loyalty for effect. Therefore hear me, ye President and other Reprobates of the upper and nether millstones, whose business which is to grind with steady continuality those who are guilty of misfortune.

So give ear, you who have ears in abundance, to this my loyal complaint. I have been outraged — victimized — destroyed. Warped in my liberties and demoralized in my pursuits, I now demand the protection of Congress.

One summer day I left the grottos of New Hampshire, to travel South. Two hundred men who wanted to get rid of me signed a paper as to my worth, and, with the proceeds of the contribution-plate one Sabbath, I lit out. Miles I wandered, by sea and land, till I pierced the heart and borders beyond the rebellious land in the South!

One day I was walking along the road in Texas, when I saw a man in a field, with a mule and a plow and a tattered suit of gray, making believe he was at work. When I saw him in those whipped garments, my hair clove to the roof of my mouth, and my tongue got upon its end like squills in fretful turpentine. I thought of the way he had murdered our innocents, prolonged the war, starved us at Andersonville, cheated Banks on Red River, and sold cotton to our Northern Generals! My poor heart did seethe and bile, like soap in a new kettle. At last I got over the apology for a fence, and approached the villain, and said unto him in a loud, loyal tone of voice, so his mule could hear me:

"Plowin', are ye? Why ain't ye in a grocery, hurrahin' for Grant? Is this the way you spit upon your benefactors? Plowin', are ye? Why don't you leave this work for the poor blacks?"

"Nothing to pay them with!" said he.

Then I said, says I:

"You are a liar and a rebel! That old coat was not made in New England!"

He looked at me and to his mule, and said:

"Whoa, Butler!"

He had but one arm; then I knew he was a rebel, and I thought proper to subdue his rebellion. I engaged him, but alas! *he bounced me!* He thrust his one fist into my left eye; he punched me on the end of my nostril, and he kicked at me with the ungodly vehemence of a jackass. So I was compelled to move on in sorrow and suffering. He is not whipped yet! A kind negro lady kept me all night, and, because I was sore, torn, bruised, and battered, put me in her little bed. In the language of Absalom, when he hung himself by the hair up to dry, I groaned:

> "This is the place I long have sought,
> And weeped because I found it not!"

Will Congress protect her loyal citizens from such outrages?

Ku-Klux!

Again your petitioner puts forth. Walking one day in Louisiana, I saw a horse kick a gentleman of color—of Baez complexion. Of course, the gentleman was loyal; the horse was not. So I went up to him, and said to him:

"Wounded and outraged brother, who owns that horse?"

"Marsa Robert."

"Was that horse in the Southern army?"

"Yes, marsa."

"Go home, mutilated citizen; I will punish this noble brute!"

To punish him for kicking my brother, I enticed him under and between me, and, with a stout switch, so warmed the steed that he ran fifteen miles before I could stop him. I pulled up at a grocery, and who should come out from that 'ere sinful place but the man who owned the horse!

Instead of staying at home and doing his work, he had left it to niggers, and a horse to abuse them. I told him of it—told how it was my duty to protect the down-trodden and punish their oppressors. The man was a rebel; I know it, for his hair was gray! He seized the horse, hove me from its back, and, with the aid of some ungodly ones, so set upon me that I was bounced again!

Ku-Klux! Will Congress not interfere, or will it not?

Hear me again, most noble President. Not liking the rebellious atmosphere of Louisiana, I sought the everglades of Florida; and here again my loyalty caused me much suffering.

On a circus-day, while the tent was going up, I saw many contrabands seated in shady places, playing Old Sledge, Penny-Ante, and such wicked games. Procuring a box, I mounted myself thereon, and said unto these innocent men and brothers:

"Come here, sable objects of our Government, and give heed unto my advice. Behold in me a loyal man from New England! During the war I wept for you often and often. During the war I fought copperheads and butternuts, traitors and Democrats in the North, oftentimes in one day slaying ten thousand or more with my good right arm. Now I come to you from the best Government in the world, to say to you this:

"Continue as you are continuing. For years you were forced to labor, and now it is your turn to live in idleness. Make your old masters support you. Every mother's son of you here is entitled to forty acres and a mule; or, if the land is not handy, forty mules and an acre! It is your business now to govern. It is your business to make laws, and to punish the white trash of the country, turned over to your hands for

"Procuring a box, I mounted myself thereon, and said unto these innocent brothers——"—*See page* 84.

punishment by the loyal Government of the North.

"Therefore I say unto ye, sable denizens, whenever you see a white man, go for him; relieve him of his chickens, his horses, his property generally; and, if he objects, go for him in the dead hour of night, till he shall learn that you are the monarchs of America, and that——"

Just then, Mr. President, I was seized with a sudden fear. In the crowd I saw a white man loading a shot-gun. The man was seventeen feet high, and I know it, and his gun was eighty-six feet long! While he was putting seven or eight pounds of buck-shot in the left-hand barrel, I noticed a reliable contraband making haste through the crowd, coming with vigilance toward my platform. He approached, lifted his lips to my ear, and whispered:

"You'd better git; dat ar man am a Ku-Klux!"

I got!

Again was I outraged in North Carolina. While seated by the roadside, counting up spoons, watches, picture-frames, celery-dishes, punch-ladles, and such little things I had found in my travels through the country—while preparing to box and ship them to friends in the North — I saw a crowd of boys and girls coming toward me. They were children ranging from seven to twelve years of age. I looked, Mr. President and Members of Congress, upon their faces, but there was no sadness there! The little rebels were laughing and playing just like other children—and the American flag floating only thirty miles away! Great God! Mr. President, can such things be, and be tolerated in this free country? My spirit again rose within me, and my blood took unto itself feelings of vengeance. When this regiment of young rebels came along, I rose in my dignity, pulled my hat well down upon my head, stretched forth my right hand, and proclaimed:

"Oh, ye little whelps of ungodly peoplehood! Your fathers were rebels, and ye deserve death. Know ye not that I am a loyal man, and that your smiles, your laughs, your hilarious fun, and your mirth as ye are going to school, is an outrage in my ears?

"Ye know what ye are—ye are the advance-guard of Ku-Klux! Your mission is to waylay strangers, that your biggers and your backers may come up and bounce them. Why are ye not mixing with the little innocent blacks? Your fathers were thieves; they were rebels; they objected when the cross-eyed patriots of the North stole spoons; they found fault with the Christians of the country for burning houses where your rebellious, ungodly parents lived. And your mothers, what are they, O ye brats of the South? What are your mothers? They are she-adders; they are rebels; they are not so good as the blacks; and yet, ye little scapegraces dare stand up and look an honest man like me in the face!"

Becoming excited, I waved my carpet-bag, when one of the urchins, a villanous-faced youth of eleven years, sang out:

"Oh, boys! he's a carpet-bagger. We've heard just such talk before. Let's bounce him!"

And, Mr. President, they proceeded at once to carry their infernal threat into execution. They attacked me in front and rear with stones. They called me vile names. They wrenched from me my carpet-bag, and divided my plunder among them. They said I was a thief. They advised me to get to my home. I called upon several intelligent contrabands who were near to come to my relief, but so terror-stricken were they that they dare not. Dear creatures! they did not wish to plunge the country into another war! They were afraid of these young rebels; and for the sake of appearances, and to cultivate the friendship of those they feared, they stood afar off, and laughed and clapped their hands, and the urchins continually assailed me. They parted my coat-tails from the upper portion of the garment. They rolled me in the mud, and sifted sand in my hair! They put a split stick upon my nose, and turpentine-wax in my ears. But, thank God! Mr. President, they could not seal my mouth that it should not cry out against the horrible outrages inflicted upon the loyal people of the South by the Ku-Klux!

Is there no redress for patriotism? Are loyal men to be thus outraged? If so, it were better for this Government that a mill-stone were tied in its coat-tail pocket, and it be sunk in a tan-vat!

Ku-Klux!

Your petitioner therefore prays that he may be appointed the head of a commission to go South at the expense of the working people of the North, escorted by a few thousand troops armed with munitions of war and presents for the negroes, that the white rèbels who have bounced me so unmercifully may be punished, and the innocent contrabands rewarded for their generous defence of a loyal citizen. And your petitioner will ever pray, &c.

CHAPTER XI.

GOING TO THE CIRCUS.

I HAVE found a gig-gig-gift for my gig-gig-girl,
I have found a rare pup-pup-place now for fuf-fuf-fun!
I'll sh-sh-shingle my head of each curl,
And bub-bub-buy a ticket for the circus when done!

I'll walk with my gig-gig-gig-girl in the tent,
When the man with his sh-sh-show comes to town
For to have lots of fuf-fuf-fun I am bent,
And tit-tit-tit-to laugh at the tricks of the clown.

My gig-gig-girl shall gig-go with me there,
And sis-sis-sit by my side all the while!
And we'll shout and we'll coo like a pup-pup-pair
Of mud turtle did-did-doves on a stile!

We'll see the fuf-fuf-fine horses go round,
Like lightning inside the big rir-rir-rir-ring!
And laugh when the tit-tit-tumblers fuf-fuf-fall down,
To bub-bub-bounce up again with a spring.

And the woman wh-wh-what walks up the small wire,
As an ant woo-woo-would walk up a string,
As high as a sis-sis-steeple, or higher,
Indeed its a mum-mum-most wonderful thing!

We'll hear the Band sweetly pip-pip-pip-play,
Most beautiful mum-mum-music and tunes,
And stare at the tremendous did-did-display
Of fuf-fuf-fuf-fine actors, horses, and buffoons!

CHAPTER XII.

AMONG THE ASTROLOGISTS.

WE read in the newspapers that Madame Ray, on Mott street, was a very learned woman, the seventh daughter of a seventh daughter, and thither we repaired. Mott street is in New York city. It is delightfully situated between donkey-carts, dirty-faced children, and irregular-shaped dwellings. As for smells—well, a person should be suited there, as a separate and distinct smell came from around each house.

"MDM. RAY, &C."

A two-story brick house, green blinds in front, black walnut door-knob, yellow door two steps from the ground, entrance immediately from the walk. There being no bell, we knocked. As we did not knock very loud, there came no response, so we knocked again.

"Mag-g-g-g-g! The door!"

In obedience to a "C-sharp" voice, there came pattering downstairs two feet. The door opened slowly, and a red head belonging to a freckle-faced, square-faced, fat-faced, grinning-faced, dirty-faced female girl of about twenty summers and somewhere near that many winters, inserted itself outward nigh as far as the shoulders. She was very muscular about the—the—the—the chest, and we thought some of turning back, but she asked:

"Did yer knock?"

"To be s-s-s-sertainly! Is Madame Ray in?"

"She is. Walk in."

We entered. The several-faced girl closed the door, which locked itself, and led the way up stairs. She opened the door, and said, "Reception-room!" We entered, and sat down. It was a small room, about twelve feet square. A three-ply carpet on the floor, two sofas, three chairs, a table, two steel-plate engravings, a small mirror, and a photograph of a big-whiskered man, completed the useful and ornamental furniture.

From an adjoining room there came a sound of clashing dry-goods and rustling of crockery, and in two minutes or so the reddish-top called us to see the object of our search. A well-furnished room about twelve by twenty. Brocatelle curtains rather the worse for wear. A bureau on which was a pier-glass and a large bouquet. Side-table covered with books. On the wall hung a large printed and colored chart some three feet square; on this chart were innumerable figures of all colors, circles, triangles, signs, cosines, hieroglyphics, &c. On a dressing-case stood perfumery of several kinds; while a gammon-board, a set of chess-men, and a pack of cards on a stand, showed that the occupant was evidently *game.* On a well-worn mohair-covered sofa sat, as we entered, Madame Ray, who arose very gracefully to receive us. She was about forty-five years of age, red-faced, red-necked as far as we could see—and that was far enough She had brown hair, fat fingers, fat face, and fat sides. Her dress was a morning-gown of red silk, and we set her down as the worst old talker in the business.

"Good morning, fair stranger!"

"Good morning, Madame!"

"What is the object of your visit this morning?"

"We came, Madame, to consult you as to the past, the present, and the future. Having doubts in our mind as to what course to pursue, we come to you for advice and counsel."

"Have you faith?"

"Exceeding great of it!"

"Stranger, you have done well to consult me.

I know your past, and can read your future. I am gifted above all mortals, and will tell thee truly. For all this I ask but one dollar in advance. Would you know more?"

We handed her a $ on the Katanyan Bank. She returned it. We handed her a dollar on a New York Bank, which she took, and said:

"The first bill is not good here. Look out, or sharpers will put bad money on you; and that *Kat*-an-*yan* Bank is Western, and is not worth much here!"

We looked at the "gay deceiver," folded it carefully, and laid it away, first thanking the Madame. As she knew worthless money, our faith in her power increased!

"In what year was you born, sir?"

"Don't know—am an orphan who never knew nothing much!"

"What is your birthday?"

"Don't know; my parents left me their only child when I was a suckling!"

"Poor boy! Let me look at your hand. (She looked.) Now on that chart place your finger on a red number. (We put it on 2.) Now on a green one. (We put it on 9.) Now on a blue one. (We picked out 8.) Now on a yellow one. (We picked out 4.) Now, in that circle, at the top, pick out a number—any one. (We put our finger on 11.) That will do; now sit down."

We did as directed, when she said:

"Nine times two are eighteen; eight times four are thirty-two. The year you were born was 1832, and it was in the eleventh month, or December. You first put your finger on 2, then on 11, which makes your birthday the 13th."

As this was our birthday in reality, we felt a little curious to have her go on. She continued:

"You don't look so old, but you be! I can tell everything. Cut those cards. (We cut at the queen of diamonds.) You first loved a woman who was rich. She loved you, (cut again,) but she was foolish, and didn't marry you. (Cut again.) She married another, and often thinks of you, and is unhappy. (Cut again.) You married another woman. You have one child. It is a young child. (Cut again.) You will have a second wife, and she will have two children—a boy and girl. You will be very happy all your life, except a little trouble for a year. Then you will be happy, and do well. Now draw ten cards out of this pack." We did so. She continued, as she looked them over one by one:

"You have had much trouble in business, but you will come out all right before long. You are in business somewhere now, and making money. In a short time you will make more. You face up a long journey, but no danger. You are very lucky and independent. You cut the queen of hearts; you will soon meet the one you love best of all. You have some enemies, but they are afraider of you than you be of them. One of them is a dark-complexioned man with a scar on his face. He will try to kill you if you meet in the woods where he can't be seen. He is a coward, and you will not be afraid of him. The other enemy is a fat man who wants to rob you. He can't do it; you have friends who won't let him. You own land and machinery of some kind. You have an interest in some kind of a boat, which is in danger of being seized. You will have much property left you in a few years, and you are going to travel, and write books. Please open that red book on the stand, and hand it to me."

We opened the book as directed, when she continued:

"You will be an old man, and have many friends when you die, and you will die in your own house. You will die in the parlor, on a bed so you can see the sun go down. You will have friends by you, and will die very easy—just like going to sleep. You will leave property to your family. Do you wish to ask me any questions?"

"I do."

"Will it rain to-day?"

"Will it rain? That's a funny question!—nothing to do with the matter; but I don't think it will. Anything else?"

"Nothing, Madame! Good morning!"

"Good morning, sir!"

And the red-haired girl showed us out.

CHAPTER XIII.

THE RESULT OF MY COURTSHIP.

I ALWAYS was a bashful boy! Modesty wanted a depot, and used me! But I loved the fair sex, and thought to marry, in time. Funny acknowledgments to make; but, as gray hairs have bivouacked all over my head, it makes no difference if I do own up.

I tried sparking, once; it came nigh bursting me, and that idea was abandoned. Two years my lass-orated heart was like Mrs. Rachel's babies—without comforters.

Then I grew lonesome. The sun didn't look

so bright as it was. The moon looked speckled-like, as does a fellow's black pants after milking! The grass wa'n't as green. The trees wa'n't as straight. The roosters, geese, turkeys, ducks, and other "feathered songsters of the glen," did not warble as sweetly as once!

My hair grew long, and it was because I was lonesome. I was like a tree in the woods. I had been blown over by my feelings, and if I didn't "lodge," I'd fall, sure pop!

Salina Jane took my eye. She was tall as the daughters of Nathal, and more beautiful. Her father had been a rich man, and Salina Jane had a good figure—nigh onto $30,000, or less. Not being a slubberdegullion, the filthy dross had no charms for me. Salina Jane had. We looked at each other a few times. Mutuality was in the glances of each. I loved the fair Salina Jane. Salina Jane loved me, and I loved Salina Jane.

Says I, "May I?"

Says she, "To be sure—and come early!"

I went, and she was there.

It was night. The pale moon was up and doing. The little cross-eyed stars were laughing at each other, and Salina Jane and I were in the parlor. It had a stove—and a lounge—and a clock—and a table—and a yellow dog under it—and a picture of Noah and his relatives moving into their new boarding-house! And it had a carpet—and lots of chairs—and an oil lamp—and a picture of General Putnam backing his horse up a ledge of rocks. And it had in it Salina Jane and I! Often went I there, and often was Salina Jane made happy by my coming. It was years ago, but I remember well. We got to liking each other. Then it took deeper root, and we loved.

We didn't do nothing—Salina Jane and I didn't—only court each other. We used to sit and hold on to each other's hands as though we were afraid of falling out! Then we'd look at each other and smile a sweet little laugh, just as easy like! Then we'd move around on our seats, and lean on to each other, and say nothing. When we said nothing, the folks in the house wouldn't hear us, and we didn't have anything to take back.

Then the oil would give out, and it would be dark. Once I went to whisper in her ear, and she turned her head around, so that, by mistake, I whispered in her pretty mouth. This proved to be a good way to whisper, and we done it that way quite often!

Then we'd talk. I don't know what we talked about, but we talked. I didn't say much, nor Salina Jane didn't, but we said a little something every time! All winter I courted her. I thought of marrying her, but couldn't get to the sticking point no-way. Dear me, I was too bashful!

One night Salina Jane was cutting rags for a carpet. I helped her rip up a pair of her dad's old trousers, and we courted while she cut. As the long strips of rags unwound themselves from her shears, I moved myself up to her. I put my head in her lap. Salina Jane kept on cutting. I didn't know what to do, so I laid still, and she kept on cutting rags. I lay there and went to sleep. When I woke up, she had cut half my hair off by carelessness. I could stand that; she was such a sweet girl, my Salina Jane was, so it didn't make me mad. She wasn't as sweet as some girls, but she was good enough for a bright, intelligent boy as I was.

Over a year we did thusly. Three nights in the week beside Sunday, till day broke, would we sit and court. It was sweet. Never knew of anything like it. Never courted before. Sorry we hadn't. It was so nice to hitch up to Salina Jane, and at last just touch her store-clothes! How it made our back-bones jingle when our hands met! Never would have done so, if courting wasn't nice. Over another year Salina Jane and I courted. We used, the second year, to stay in the house till midnight in the summer. Then I'd get up to go. We'd go out by the gate, and spend an hour there. Then I would leave for my humble roof.

I used to buy nice things for her—molasses candy, little candy hearts, peppermint-drops, and such good stuff; apples, two for a cent apiece, and oranges without a speck of rotten in 'em! They were all for Salina Jane, and I didn't care for the expense.

Then I used to dream of her. I'd think myself a fish, and Salina Jane and I would sport among the waters, and she'd chase me around by the stones and old roots, and under the soddy banks of the creek where I thought we were. Then I'd dream we were little warbling birds, and sitting on a high limb of a tall tree together, sweetly singing! Then I'd dream I was a horse, drawing a nice carriage in which was Salina Jane! Then, when, after working hard all day, I'd eat a hearty supper of pigs' feet, cold potatoes, and such light food, and have a night-mare, and dream Salina Jane was on my chest, working butter! If I hadn't loved that girl, she'd never laid so heavy on my heart!

Over two years I courted and she courted. It was my first real experience. I always wanted to marry Salina Jane, but dare not ask her for fear she'd say No. Over two years I lavished on that gushing girl sweetmeats, new raisins, the first green apples of the season, and young wintergreens, with a prodigal hand.

One day a platter-headed lawyer came along. He was just sweet flag, done up in sugar-coated cakes! He saw Salina Jane afar off, and made for her. He was a gay and festered chap. He knew more than he'd forgot—a heap more. He wore store-clothes on week-days! I didn't. He had the advantage of me there. He hadn't brains enough to keep his hair straight, so it curled. Salina Jane liked curly hair!

He carried a watch—an Egyptian bull's-eye,

plated with gold! It was a big thing. I had no watch! Salina Jane went back on me, and made for the watch. He had a roll of counterfeit money, and he showed her the end of it. She thought he was hefty about the purse, but he wasn't—nor about the head either! He called with a carriage—livery carriage—and they went out riding. It was the night I was to sit up with Salina Jane. I went there to her domicile, but she had gone.

"O Salina Jane,
Don't do it again!"

I wrote in a bold hand on the 10 x 12 mirror which hung in the parlor, with a piece of tallow, and left the house. I went off to weep, and for two hours my affections oozed out of my eyes as water would ooze out of a wet sponge with a big man sitting on it! She read the poetry, but didn't give no heed!

Poor Salina Jane! She was deceived in that man, and *I* knew it. He wasn't what he was cracked up to be, and *he* knew it! Gradually, as sparks fly upward, she left me to mourn, and I done it. Two years and three months, by the almanac, had I courted her, good and strong; but she left honest worth for a plated watch and curly hair.

I felt bad! Whenever she'd sit on the fence, as she used to at times, after driving the pigs out of her folks' cornfield, I used to watch her. When she'd get off the fence and go in the house, I'd go and sit on the spot she had sat on. For a while it calmed my heart and made me feel good. But she got thicker and thicker with her new lover, and, after a while, sitting on the fence failed to relieve me!

Well, matters grew worse. That fellow put in his best licks, and told Salina Jane all manner of foolish yarns—got her all manner of fancy jiggeretts for keepsakes, and I was left to mourn the loss of time, money, and affection, to say nothing of blasted hopes. How I'd courted her!

Day and night I had made love unto her, and she had led me, poor, guileless boy, as a butcher does a calf! But it was soon to end. My egg-shell of happiness had squshed in my hand, and the yolk of it run all over my heart.

In two weeks this fellow and Salina Jane were married. He was older than I—was born first—but I spoke to him about it just as though we were of the same age. Anger abided in my heart when I spoke to him. I demanded satisfaction—not the satisfaetion I had looked for with Salina Jane as Mrs. "B." P., but the satisfaction a gentleman should expect. He looked at me kind of pityingly when I spoke of it, and said he'd pay me.

"Pay for what?" said I—"for a busted heart—for all my spare time—for my candy—my sweetmeats—my raisins—my big apples, and all the presents I have given Salina Jane?"

"No," said he; "but I'll pay you for courting her up so nice; *it just saved me the trouble!*"

And that was all the satisfaction I got.

CHAPTER XIV.

THE CONFIDING WIDOW.

ON the train, and sitting in front of us, was a middle-aged lady, who all of a sudden turned about, and asked:

"Are you a Baptist?"

"Yes; I believe in the *dip*-theory!"

"Well, I thought so; you look just like a Baptist minister I knew once, or at any rate I heerd preach in Rochester, New York, and I didn't know but you was him."

"I never preached in *Rochester*."

"Did you ever preach in Lockport?"

"No; I never preached in any of the *Eastern* cities."

"I suppose it keeps you busy preaching out here! I've heern that there was some good preaching done here. I live in Rochester. I'm a Baptist, too, and I think that it is the best church in the world."

"Yes, it is a good church—a large and prosperous church."

"Yes, it is. I've been visiting in Milwaukee and it seems as if there wa'n't much religion in Milwaukee; and I'm so glad I met you! Somethin' told me you was a Baptist preacher, and I'm so glad I've met you! What may I call your name?"

"Knubson—Ezekiel Knubson."

"I never heern tell of that name; but I've heerd of Mr. Spurgeon, an Englishman."

"No relation, madam. I'm a Norwegian."

"Where is your field?"

"In La Crosse, Wisconsin."

"Oh, yes! I've heern tell of that place. I've read in the newspapers about a wicked man who lives there."

"That's the place."

"Well, now, I'm real glad I met you! I always meet somebody wherever I go. I have a girl twelve years old; she j'ined the Baptist church last year. Her name is Matilda Parkhurst. My name is Parkhurst. My husband was Deacon Parkhurst. He died last Spring. I am a widow now, and have got a nice farm near Rochester. I had a house in Rochester, but I sold it for nine hundred dollars, and had the money stolen from my pocket by somebody on the cars. I think I know who stole it, but I can't tell, for I couldn't find him. A man saw me buy a ticket, and he came and sat in the seat with me. He said he was a Baptist, and I told him all about things. Purty soon he said he had the nose-bleed, and he went out to wash his nose in a place where we stopped to wood, and the cars started before he got his nose washed! He said I must look out for my money. And I told him it was safe in my pocket. Then he said, if I saw a red-headed man with a red moustache and a silver-headed cane come along, I must look out for him. Purty soon I saw a man with a red head and a mustache come through the cars, but he had left his cane. He walked on past me—didn't hardly look at me nor mother. After he had gone out of the car I felt for my pocket-book, and it was gone. Then I told the conductor I'd been robbed by the red-haired man, and he went and brought him back; and I told the folks in the car what the Baptist man told me about looking out for such men, and how he put his handkerchief to his nose and went out, 'way back on the road. The red-headed man said he was a member of the Legislature, and he told his name, and said he wouldn't steal; and he got mad at the conductor, and said I was an old fool, and all the folks laughed, and he said the man with the nose-bleed had robbed me, and he made them believe it; but I knew better, 'cause he was such a nice man, and he bought a lot of hickory-nut meats and put them in my pocket for me, and I've got some yet. Won't you have some, Brother Knubson?"

"Ah, thank you; just a few."

"And you never got your money?"

"No. Ain't it a shame, now!"

"And your girl, Matilda—she joined the church?"

"Yes; last year she was baptized."

"Where was she baptized?"

"In the river."

"Ah! What month was she baptized in?"

"In May—on the fourteenth day of May."

"Well, May is a good month to be baptized in."

"Yes, so it is. And Matilda so enjoyed it! After she was converted she writ some verses about her father's death. Lemme see—yes—no—yes, this was the way they begin:

> " 'Dear father, you had to die
>   Before I was but eleven,
> And I am goin now to try
>   To meet you up in Heaven.

That was the first verse:

> " 'What made you go away,
>   And leave me here behind you?
> But I have been converted
>   And some day will come and find you.'

That was the second verse. There was three.

> " 'And now I've lost my father,
> And I haven't any brother,
> And as you have gone to Heaven
> I'll have to stay with mother!' "

This was the last verse. Matilda has writ a good many verses. I wish I had some for you to read! She writ a hymn, but I can't sing it without somebody to start it. [We offered to start it, but she had forgotten the words.] I never could sing, unless my husband, Deacon Parkhurst, started it. He was a powerful starter! Didn't you never hear of him? He made stickin'-salve, and had a big farm. He was a good man, too. He never scolded back when I scolded."

"Did he die?"

"Law, yes! and I'm his widow. He died one night, as easy!"

"Was he resigned?"

"Oh, yes; he was one of the willingest men to die I ever seen!"

"*I have no doubt of it!* And you have not married again?"

CHAP. XV.

TO A BRIGHT-EYED MAIDEN.

WHEN the lamp low down is turned,
And at your feet a lover "lies"
Telling how his love is spurned—
How his heart for you now dies!
Watch his eye—read it right,
Treacherous is its changing light.

When he pleads, and says his sorrow
Will be greater than can be borne;
Bid him wait—perhaps to-morrow
Will bring to each a different morn.
Watch his eye—read it right—
Test his love for you to-night.

When he talks of love and wedlock—
  Offers you his heart and hand;
Know ye that each are honest—
  His may be siege most boldly planned!
      Watch his eye—read it right—
      Many a maiden lost to-night!

Is he true and noble-hearted?
  Learn this, maiden, ere you wed—
Else you sorrow till the dawning
  Of the day beyond the Dead!
      Search his heart—read it right—
      Joy or sorrow from to-night!

Many prizes may be offered—
  Many traps to catch your beauty;
Many gifts in *words* be proffered—
  Gently maiden—life's a *duty*,
      Answer not—another night
      You may read by clearer light.

When you know he's true and noble,
  Look forever in his eyes.
If your *heart* then bids you love him,
  Live and love—enjoy the prize.
      Trust him ever—bless the night
      You learned to read his heart aright.

"Tavern's all full," said the clerkist as he looked at Clorinda.—*See page* 123.

CHAPTER XVI.

EXPERIENCE IN BOSTON AT THE PEACE BANJOREE.

WE took her there—Clorinda Magwilligan, chief daughter and delayed spinster of the house of Magwilligan, of Magwilligansville.

We have known Clorinda long. She was a tall girl, and meant it. All tall girls mean it. They mean to be long for this world. So did Clorinda. Years ago we loved her. Twenty years ago we climbed up about her neck and hung a few lusciousary kisses on her triumphant lips. And when her eyes beheld the sweet glory of our coming down past the barn where the cows were milked by Clorinda, as she sat squatted on a one-legged stool, the eyelight of her aforesaid eyes would glimmer, the freckles on her face would seem illuminated, and she'd always give us a kiss, milk or no milk.

She was a healthy kissist, full of gentle and stimulating vigor.

Did you ever kiss a girl and fairly hanker for more? We loved her, and she loved back. We planted kisses, and love sprouted till the branches thereof made a grove under which we took refuge.

Clorinda heard of the Peace Banjoree in Boston. She wanted to go. We took her there. Went on an excursion tour. Weather hotter than making tomato pickles. We rode in the cars and on a boat, then went on foot. Clorinda wears No. 7s, small. She had understanding to let.

Gracious! but didn't she sling style! Such a Grecian bend! And her waterfall—right on the upper end of her head, like froth on soda-water. And a bonnet twice the size of a postage-stamp—a three-cent one at that! And a dress whose trail outrivalled the lateral extension of the peacock, and more grandly gorgeous!

We put up at a hotel about ten minutes. "Tavern's all full," said the clerkist, as he looked at Clorinda. She was a tower—that is, we looked up to her. She said, "Move on." We walked to another hotel, asked the same question, and the same clerk said they was all full. Then he told us to go to the "Tremont." There we went. Walked afoot. Went straight ahead on a curve. Came to the "Tremont." The same clerk was there. Said he was full. And he looked at Clorinda. Then he told us to go to the "American." So we patted it around there. Saw the same clerk. He said they was all full. Told us to go to the "Parker House," and we started to find it, but couldn't do it. Come to find out, 'twas the "Parker House" we had entered every time; and that clerk knew, when he told us to find the house we were in, the streets were so dyrned crooked we couldn't! Clorinda and I moved on. We walked all over the city, on the same street. We asked a policeman where was a hotel, did he know? And he said there wa'n't none, for it was Banjoree week. He asked if we had heard the big organ, or seen Gilmore? We said No. We went to find O. and G., the twin celebrities of Boston. We went up to Bunker Hill Monument. Didn't know but Clorinda and us could bunk there. But the Monument was all taken up. Somebody told us that Warren fell over there. We went to see, but he had got up and gone!

Then we went to Breed's Hill. We wanted to see Grant, and, knowing his love for dogs, thought to find him at Breed's! But he wa'n't there; a Boston Peace Banjoree Yankee had hired him for a tobacco-sign! So we didn't know which one was Grant, they were so plenty!

Tramping around, Clorinda blistered her feet. She was not used to walking. She was brought up in Rhode Island, and hadn't room to turn her feet. We couldn't walk, so we stood still till the Coliseum came around.

It was a big thing. Clorinda got all jammed up. She was made thinner nor a lath. When I hugged her, it seemed like squeezing a paper-folder. But she was good! We heard the big organ. We saw Gilmore counting his money. Hotel accommodations being out of the question, we anchored under a tree. Country taverns don't contain too much! After Clorinda had her head blowed full of sweet discordancies and St. Vitus' melodies, I took her down on the Common, and paid five dollars for an hour in the arms of Morpheus. Clorinda was there too.

We had a fine supper—two peanuts and a boiled bean split. Only a dollar! And then we had refreshments—two pints of water, with yellow paper in for lemonade, at two shillings a glass.

And such a breakfast—soup made from the back of a postage-stamp! I had to take Clorinda off that diet; she was getting fat. Only cost twenty-eight dollars a day to see the big organ and Deacon Gilmore, chief of the Boston banditti!

Clorinda was sweet, for certain! I filled her full of molasses-candy and gingerbread the first day, but the stamps gave out. They called it a Peace Jubilee, and took the last piece I had—except Clorinda. But we saw the Banjoree, and shall die happy, if not sooner. Clorinda was demoralized. Some wretch sat down on her bandbox. It caved in, and up went her bonnet.

But we saw the Peace Banjoree, and Gilmore, and the big organ. Clorinda had her feet trod on in the crowd more nor a thousand times. I thought they were her tally-books. And she lost her trail. I'm sorry about that! But I didn't lose Clorinda. I looked up to her so much, it was no trouble to look her up!

Clorinda never was so badly jammed up. I think she was hugged by three thousand men whose habits were good, and by seventeen thousand whose habits were t'otherwise. She was squeezened out flat one way, and squeezened up flat t'other way. And she never would have been so long in the first place, if it had not been for the huggings I had given her when she was little. When you see a little short, fat girl, it is a sign she has not been properly hugged. If she had, it would have squeezed her up taller! But then, we saw the Peace Jamboree, and we heard the music. And such music! It seemed as if all the fiddlers, and feline-intestine scrapers, and mashers of base drums, and blowers through brass instruments, had all the blacksmith-shops, tin horns, dogs with kettles tied to their tails, children who had partaken of too much small-beer, men with the toothache, cats on wood sheds, serenaders on a bender, fire-crackers, pistols, muskets, rat-traps on a drunk, music run mad, and harmony badly bust, had contrived on this occasion to fill Clorinda's ear with the most unmitigated doings!—and had succeeded. Clorinda had so much in her ear, that I could not whisper love in it in a fortnight. I bought a tin horn and whispered through that. But it was no use.

The only way I could bring her to her senses, or tone her auricular appurtenances down to their original condition, was to seat her on a railroad engine and let her whistle it six hours a day until she recovered. But she has not been good-natured a day since. That bran-new frock with streaks up and down it, is all skurypt, till the continuation of her trail resembles a garbage-cart struck by lightning while blessed with a full load.

And that little bonnet she had—a hundred and sixteen dollars' worth of style and ten cents' worth of fabric! Oh, I guess not! Four firkins of butter to buy a bonnet, besides the other firkins disposed of to purchase other wardrobe for Clorinda. You see, she was a dairyman's daughter! Linked sweetness long drawn out, or butter long a-coming! And that little ridicule she had to carry powder, white chalk, and red doin's, and those little scrambled hair-things what they wear, and some other devices, continuations, and inventions not enumerated—somebody sat down on it, and when they rose, it resembled a sum in multiplication attempted by a boy who did not know how!

Clorinda says Peace Jamborees are a humbug We reached her home, the Lord only knows how. The Banjoree busted my çash, exhausted my patience, destroyed my raiment, upset my health, deprived me of rest. During all the time it continued, Clorinda and I got no sleep except when I took her down on the Common, where we reposed like two doves with but a single stamp, two sweethearts piled as one, under the shadow of a tree which loomed up against the State House. I wanted them to let me rock Clorinda to sleep in the cradle of liberty, but they said the cradle was full.

I don't want her photograph taken now. It ain't purty. She don't look good-natured. I don't believe her picture would call sweetness back to sour milk. I felt very sad about it. The juice of gladness doth not abound in my heart. The permeating sap of contentment rangeth not around my gizzard, as was its wont. I left Clorinda at the house of her paternal derivative, and returned, put on my good clothes, and went to see her. But she was not seeable. She was getting fixed. So I sat myself down under her window, and plaintively I sighed out:

"Oh, Clorinda, 'Rinda, 'Rinda, draw nigh—do!"

But she wouldn't. And then the pale moon scooted along, and I said:

"Oh, moon, moonie, moonie, pity my woe—do, just once!"

But he wouldn't. And a little star followed the moon like a poodle-dog follows a little girl, and I said:

"Oh, star, starie, starie, twinkle me one—do come and pin my love onto 'Rinda's heart!"

But nary a twinkle. And a cloud hegiraed overhead, seeming not to care a dyrn for my trouble; and in the agony of my bitterness I sank back upon the grass, and said:

"Oh, cloud, cloudie, flying cloudie, cloud me no more, for my heart can't stand it!"

And I called again to Clorinda, and she would not come. And it is all on account of the Peace Jamboree. She was the best-natured girl on the creek till this transpired. She was sweeter than shrimps, or a free ride to a picnic. But, alas! her sweetness is departed. What with the jamming and the cramming, the eating of old baked beans, second-hand peanuts, and gingerbread whereon many an army of flies had camped, she wasn't well!

She says, No more excursion for her! She did not like the Hub. She prefers to remain in the dignity of her own domicile, to take care of the little doings thereof; so she goeth not to Boston for another spree, not even to see the Coliseum, or the big organ, or the crooked streets, or Gilmore, or any of them things; but she goeth to bed in madness and in sadness, but not in any gladness.

Such is Clorinda; while I am disconsolate, used up, out of cash. But, thank the Lord, I have helped Gilmore, have an interest in the Coliseum, heard the big organ, and have been to Boston!

CHAPTER XVII.

MY WIDOW IN THE PARK.

RIGHT down there—just where it was last year.

O Park! Why couldn't you move away, that I be not moved by harrowing recallings in view of you? Confound you, but memory lingers with a fellow like a hole in his hat-band.

All day it had rained like much thunder, and the wet winds blew moistness all over the window and the soul. It was one of them days when a person feels just like it, and sometimes more so. So did I.

And I read in the newspaper all the political, religical, financical, nonsensical, and litterical articles it had. Then the advertisements. And this one:

"A young widow, with a loving heart and yearning soul, wishes to form the acquaintance of a nice gentleman who will love her. A good-looking man preferred. Address, appointing an interview, Rosa Morgan, Post-office."

That's me! Why not? I looked into the mirror—no reflections. Hair turning gray—but gray is becoming more fashionable than blue! Form, a little bit on the stoop—but Hogarth says a curve is a line of beauty. Not many wrinkles in the face—only ninety to the square inch—but what is wrinkles, when a widow is in the way? And a wig—but thus we encourage industry, and then we thrive.

So we wrote unto her, saying things as she reposed her eyes onto and drank into her trump of hearts. She answered back again. So did we. And missives passed between us—postage-paid. And the notes were on brass-mounted or gilt-edged paper, to betoken eclatness of design and high-bloodness of rank and style.

At last, oh! at last. When you have a bite, pull up. She, our Rosa, wanted an interview. She wrote as if we were much to her in the spirit and in the flesh. Greeting! We read her gushingness, for it yearned all over the brass-mounted paper she performed her writing onto.

So we yearned. We wrote epistles. We made little note to her. We asked her to come and meet us in the Park. Union Square Park.

At eight P.M. Sunday night. Pleasant. Indeed, mooney. At the Fifteenth street-entrance. Broadway side. And if she held our letter in her hand when she arrived, she would be known. And greeted. And loved. And why not? What is Park, and man, and folks for?

She answered Yes. She put a postscript to her catalogue of affections, which read:

"P. S.—I'll be there, sure. With the letter in left hand. Already I love you. I'll be there.

"Rosa."

Happy! As a clam with a new toothpick. Would she come? Would a woman fool a fellow? They never have yet!

So we fixed. Lie still, wriggling heart! Why those flutters, when the time will come without? We took a bath and paddled in the water an hour, dreaming of our Rosa. We had our wig brushed and ears curled. And our face shaved two layers deep below the skin. We looked rare and high-toned! Then we mounted a new hat over our head. Put on a blue neck-tie with maroon trimmings. A red silk undershirt like a lap-dog. A frilled shirt with buttons behind, so as not to unquilt the front and discomfit the starch thereon. And we put onto us sich a pair of lily-white linen pants, thin and cool. And we strode forth twenty minutes before the appointed time. We sat upon the bench. Our heart! Have you ever been there? Did you ever wait for your sweetheart, or one who might be, until your heart became like a roasted "shoo-fly" for uneasiness? Then come in!

We sat on the bench. A very hard bench for thin pants. Uneasy lies the head that wears a bench!

People passed both ways. The mosquitoes were active. They bored pneumatic tunnels into our rheumatic legs till we dogmatically cursed them much. They bit, and we slapped. We slapped, and they bit. They bored into our knee-pans, into our thighlets, and all up and down the match-shaped fatness of our calves. We endured torture, and killed the cusses by dozens. We slapped them till folks thought we were patting the juba, and till our white linen was like unto a quail's bosom filled with shot, and a red-pepper box-cover on the leak.

We killed them, and smeared their corpses over our legs like embroidery. We killed them at their meals, till the white pants were red-flecked with human gore.

O Rosa! Rosa! why dostest not come, if thou comest ever? Knowest thou not that it becometh thee to come soon? Why keep lover on a hard seat, killing mosquitoes and spoiling breeches? But we forgive thee, sweet sylphess!

At last! She came. Twenty minutes late. Forty minutes mosquito-killing! Now look at our pants! What a specledation to be in! She had our letter in her left hand. It was her. O Jupiter!—Jupe, desert us not!

But she was a charmer. Five feet ten inches high. Slim as a rail. Forty-nine years old, if a day. And her face looked like that of a trained cat—decidedly catankerous. She had her mouth in a prim. Her eyebrows blacked, and lips painted with vermilion. And a little yaller parasol. And a No. 7 boot. But she was a woman!

We weakened—then rallied and braced up. "Ah! good evening! *So* glad! How good to come! Could have waited for hours. Let us walk here and there. Let us go hence, to see how women dress and men govern. Come, Rosa, sweet!" And we ventured out from the Park. Why weep when taking medicine? Oh, young widow—with a yearning heart! Sainted wether of the flock, art thou she? But we prattled sweetly. We reached up to her arm. We were so glad she was nice! We feared she might be a squash-waisted nymph of about nine hundred. Hearts do always find their mates, and that is what she told us.

Folks laughed as we reached up to her. She was so tall, and we a little, short, fat one—she the long, and we the short of it! Oh, advertisement of yearning young widow wanting a man to love! Our thermometer left us—we grew rich—linked sweetness drawn out too long—and we wilted.

It was a pretty picture—a fine, lengthy view. We walked toward her home. We wanted to, but our heart failed us, on turtle-doving this tadpole beside us; so we invited her to a saloonery of ice-cream benevolence. We seated her on a chair. Called for two vanillas, large! Then she excused us for a moment, while we went to speak to a friend at the door. We gave a waiter a dollar, thinking that would pay for cooling her off. We saw her through the window enjoying it, and fled like Moses away from the Egyptians. Some day we shall dare to look in to see if she is there yet, or if she has found a lover.

CHAPTER XVIII.

"PARIS CLUB ROOMS."

THE poor of New York we leave behind to-night, for there is nothing attractive in the garb of necessity or misfortune, nor is there much to entice in the watery eyes and watery potatoes, the hard floor and hard bread, the whining voice or creaking hinges, the scarred countenances and ragged clothes, the dark rooms and dark life of those who are poor as the acme of poverty, and whose life is of so little account that their death and burial is almost unnoticed, except by the proper authorities.

Leave them all behind to-night.

The lamps are again lit. By the thousand they gleam and glimmer everywhere. To the right and left—up and down Broadway, to the right hand and left hand, as far as the eye can reach, they stand, better guardians of the night than many of the police officers.

Many a man in New York owes his life to the street-lamps, the steady glare of which have more terror in them for evil-doers than a score of police-clubs. The lamps never have to go in to drink, or toast their shins before the fire in some curious place around the corner, downstairs.

"Carriage, gentlemen?"

"Well, yes! Do you know where the new Paris Club Rooms are?"

"No."

"Drive to No. — East Forty-second street. And say—drive around by Riley's first."

"All right!"

And away we go up Broadway to Eighth street —down Eighth, and then to the right. How the wheels rumble over the cold pave! The horses are fast; the click of their steel-shod feet on the stones evokes sparks as we dash ahead. The carriage is well cushioned, and rides easy. We pull the furs about our ears, draw the robes over our knees, and hurry on. Who cares for carriages? Who rides in all these cars, carts, carriages, cabriolets, and coupees? Somebody! Where do they live? Somewhere! Where are they all hurrying? Somewhere—to the theatre—to the cars—the boats—to go from home—to return—to church—to fill some engagement—to anywheres and everywheres.

Here is Riley's! One of our party wants a choice Havana; another wants a little sherry; another wants to see his friends fixed. And away we go again! Still lamps, gaslight, carriages, and pedestrians. Now to the right—to the left—to the right over beyond the haunted cellar and its murder-scenes.

We stop before a four-story brown-stone front,

handsomely-planned dwelling. "No one at home?" Wait.

"Driver, it is now a quarter past eight. Return here at three in the morning—sharp!"

"Ay, ay, sir." And the carriage rumbles away where the horses can rest and the driver keep warm; for the establishment is now under pay, subject to order.

It is not a year since these club-rooms were opened. Comparatively few of New York people know of them. There is much done in New York *no one* knows of!

Up the wide stairs—three of us. A silver bell-pull. All is dark and quiet. A pull on the bell. Listen! Not a tinkle is heard. "Pull again?" No; once is enough. A bolt is withdrawn—a light chain rattles—a door swings open—a step is heard—a little wicket in the outer door is raised—the face of a stout black man looks out, but the door does not open.

"All right —— —— —— ——!"

"Certainly, gentlemen!"

The wicket closes. All is dark. Another bolt is withdrawn, and the large iron door, painted to resemble rosewood, opens silently. The ebony waiter steps back. "Good evening, gentlemen!" We enter silently. The door swings to —a large bolt returns to its socket. The inner door, also of iron, swings open—we pass in—that swings to and is bolted, and we are in the new Paris Club Rooms.

To the left, into a reception-room. Hat, furs, overcoat, and overshoes are handed to a waiter who will be there when we want them again. How elegant the room! A grate full of red coals throws out a generous warmth. A chestnut side-board in one corner of the room is covered with glasses and decanters. The polite door-tender invites us to help ourselves. We sit by the grate and are blessed with the grateful heat. While the door-tender disappears—we see him leave the room—we listen to hear his footfall;

the soft carpets are too much for us—the doors open too silently. We would not know but he stood outside the reception-room door, waiting in the hall like a black statue.

In a moment or two he returns.

"Gentlemen, whenever you are ready!"

"All right!"

We arise and follow him. How silently the doors open! How the carpets yield to pressure of the foot! Not a bit of noise—no more than if this were a deserted grave. Out in the hall—to the end thereof. Another door opens, as leaves float in the air, and we enter the *salon* proper.

What a splendid room! Full forty feet square. Three grates on three sides of the room lend a cheerful look. The carpets are of the softest texture! The chandeliers are of magnificent pattern and generous proportions, two score of gas-burners making the room light as day. And the paintings on the walls -decidedly

French in all that makes up the novel, the striking and suggestive! In the centre of the room is a faro-table, around which twenty men are sitting and standing at play. In the right-hand corner is a roulette-table, around which excited persons are betting on the red or black. On the left side of the room are smaller tables for poker, whist, cribbage, vintugn, and other games. There are five doors to the room besides the one at which we entered. There are half a dozen sofas, several easy-chairs, four tête-à-têtes, and a splendid side-board well stocked with the choicest wines, brandies, liquors, and cigars in the city. Everything denotes extravagance and excellent taste for furnishing. The furniture is of the most expensive make and elegant design. The picture-frames are of solid rosewood. The room is warm, and more than comfortable. And how still it is! No introduction is needed, though we introduce our friends to one of the proprietors, to whom we are introduced by a card and private note.

"Welcome, gentlemen! Make yourselves at home; and if anything be lacking for your comfort, it shall be sent for!"

"Ah! thanks!"

Half a dozen really beautiful ladies are sitting around the room, or lounging idly at the tables. One of them is crocheting a beautiful lap-robe, which in a few days will astonish people on the avenues. All are beautiful, painted, dressed, and accomplished, as the word goes. There are books; here is a guitar; here are silver-mounted pistols, silver goblets, riding-whips, and silver spurs hanging over a mantle.

What will you do? Would you smoke? Here is a genuine Havana. Are you thirsty? Here is wine, water, &c. Would you play faro? Here is room—always room. Would you make up a party at poker? Here are cards, table, ivory checks, and partners. Would you play cribbage? Here are cards, cribbage-board, and partners, either male or female. Would you sit by the fire and warm? No need of that, for the room is just right. Would you talk with one of the young ladies? Here is a tête-à-tête, or a sofa; yonder, in the corner, are vacant chairs; and here is a charming young lady who speaks French, Italian, Spanish, and English. She can tell you of travel, of cities, of games, of watering-places, and of people. Would you hear music from the guitar? It is but a step into another room, and you can remain there as long or short a time as you please, and she will play some low-toned, gentle tune for you; and if your head aches, hers are the fingers which will try and still the throbbing temple. Are you hungry? Step this way, into the lunch-room. Here are oysters, cold chicken, sandwiches, ale, &c., &c.; or you can wait till one o'clock, for supper. All is free—that is, in the eating and drinking line. You can play or not, as you choose. You can drink, smoke, or eat—just as you please. It costs nothing. The proprietor presses you to try a cigar. The young lady you are talking with insists on your drinking a glass of wine with her —then another—then another.

How still it is!

No loud talk—no profanity. At times an excited man at the faro-table utters a loud exclamation. The dealer looks up at him. A negro waiter asks him what he will have. He calls for a glass of liquor, and all is still again. Or some one asks the case-keeper what cards are dead and what cards are yet to be dealt out. Or some one wants another stock of "chips," as the round, flat ivory checks, about the size of half-dollar silver pieces, are called. Or some man ejaculates, "*Thunder!*" as he loses fifty or a hundred dollars. But, for all that, there is no noise.

Who are these men and women?

Never mind who! The women are somebody

—at least, they were somebody till they came here. They go to summer watering-places as somebody. They know enough of the world to convince you that they are *somebody;* but their names—ah! we forget to inquire!

"And the men?" Ah, no! people don't tell all they know. Some of these men are "sports," who live by gambling. Some of them are merchants, business men, politicans, office-holders, speculators, and a few curiosity-students like ourself.

"What do they come here for?"

What makes the wind blow—water run downhill—smoke ascend—men love women—women love men? We can't tell you? Most of them come here to gamble—to make or lose money faster than by legitimate business. We meet some of these men on Wall street—in the Custom-House. We saw three of those here tonight, on the floor of Congress lately. If you would learn their names, come here as we came, and see for yourself. It is easy to come, after you know the ropes!

Everything is extravagance and dissipation. You can get more here than we have yet spoken of, if you have money and desire. There are private rooms. Men meet here to drink wine and devise means to carry elections, to control the people, to manipulate railroad stock—to affect the market, to study on some new road to wealth. After the plans are laid, a few hundreds are lost or won at the gaming-tables; and in the early morn, after a supper fit for the gods, home is sought.

This is a modern gambling-house. There is nothing wanting to make attractive this resort of those who have money. Poor people have no business here. The handsome young ladies who are so agreeable, get a good living and wear the finest of clothing every day. There are from six to ten of these beauties here every night. They hail from other cities—are the *crême de la crême* of their sisterhood—adepts in cunning and all the arts to win man from his good resolutions, and to entice money from him. They play poker, whist, or other games, with the coolness and dexterity of an expert, and are so very interesting that a man is nearly willing to pass through the gate to perdition if she but open it for him, and, with a smile and languid eye, will start him on the downward road.

There is a selectness about this modern gambling-house. None but men who know their business ever enter here. The owners of this palace are polite, and seemingly generous. The best of everything is set before the guest—wines, food, and cigars. One o'clock at night is the hour for a most sumptuous repast, when all the delicacies of the season are served in a long dining-room, where can sit forty-four guests at the table. You get here the most tempting roasts, the fattest broiled quail and other birds, the finest oysters, fruits in and out of season, coffee of rare flavor, champagne of exquisite memory—all in abundance, served by the most attentive waiters. You can eat alone, or by the side of a lady; or you can sit outside, listen to the rattle of knives, forks, spoons, and dishes, the pop of champagne-corks, and the jokes; for every one has a license to say a good thing, if he but knows how, where, and when. For all this luxury there is no price charged. You return to the *salon* and begin again, or go home, as you please.

It is now two o'clock. There is a lull in the ivory storm. Let us try the "Tiger," as faro is called. Here is the table—a long mahogany affair, covered with green velvet, on which are glued thirteen cards—from ace to king, in two rows, six in each row, with the seven-spot by itself, at the end.

Behind this table sits the "dealer," a quick-eyed, quick-fingered, cool-nerved man, who seems like a machine in his look and motions. We will play a little, for it is not polite to run the house. At the right hand of the dealer, on the table, is a box filled with stacks of ivory checks, piled up in stacks like little plates. They are about the size of a silver dollar, if our readers can remember what size that is. They are white, red, blue, each color denoting different value. The white ones are worth a dollar each; the red ones are worth five dollars each; the blue ones are worth fifty dollars each. For fifty dollars he hands us fifty of these white checks, and puts the greenbacks into a drawer beside him under the table-top. We sit down by the table; a half-dozen men sit beside us, each with a stack of chips, white, red, or blue, as the purse of the player, or his inclination, calls for. The keen-eyed dealer opposite the table in front of us takes a full pack of cards, puts them in a silver box with an open top, so we can all see what card is first. The cards cannot fall out of the top, for there is a rim which holds them. They are kept up to the top by means of a spring in the box underneath the cards, pressing them steadily, firmly up.

"Ready!"

The first card visible to all is, we will say, a ten-spot. No one knows what the next card is. We will put ten dollars' worth of checks on the king on the table. If the first card under the ten be a king, the bank wins. The cards are drawn out one at a time, and laid in two piles regularly. The first card (under the one which is visible) is the dealer's. All money bet on that, he takes. The second card belongs to us. All can see what cards are drawn. All the little piles of ivory checks standing on the first card, of he two drawn, are picked up by the dealer and et back where they belong in the box. All the ttle piles of ivory on the next card drawn call r the dealer to set beside them a pile of corresponding size and value. We bet on the king. The game goes on—the dealer draws, takes, and pays. Hallo! The king was in his pile—we lose ten dollars! We put ten more on the same card. Next time it wins, as it comes out first or second. He now puts ten dollars more on it. We place the twenty dollars on the Jack. He deals; the first one in the pack under the king is a four-spot. He takes all there is bet on that card. The next one is a Jack. We had twenty dollars on it. He pays without a word. Perhaps half a dozen men were betting on the Jack. He pays each one all he bet thereon. We now have forty dollars. We shove the pile of chips or checks over to the queen. The rest of the players put their checks where they think best. He draws two more cards. The first is a six-spot, which loses; the second is a queen. We have again won. He places checks on these to correspond with the pile we had there. Now we have eighty dollars—having lost one bet. We pile our chips in front of us, and put twenty dollars on the nine-spot. He draws. The nine-spot comes first; we lose. It is our opinion that the nine-spot will not lose twice in succession, so we place twenty dollars more on it. Again he draws. The nine-spot wins. And so it goes. We bet on which card we please. Every other card wins for us—every other card wins for the bank.

"How do they make it pay?"

That is the great question. When two cards are together, the half of what was bet on that card—an ace, for instance, if two aces are together in the pack—is taken by the dealer, for it is called a *split*. This appears to be the only percentage the game has over those who play against it; and in large games, such as are played here, the half which the house wins on *splits* often amounts to a thousand or more dollars a night. Again, men come in, lose a hundred or two dollars, and quit. The bank is generally this much the gainer. Sometimes a man will lose a thousand, or twenty thousand dollars, a night, here. Sometimes a man will win as much; though few men have the nerve to play their "luck," as it is called, as high when winning as when losing. There is a percentage in favor of the bank—at least, a faro-bank generally wins, and they who play against it generally lose.

We started in with fifty dollars. It is now fifteen minutes of three. In fifteen minutes a carriage will be at the door. We have been lucky; in the place of fifty dollars, we have now nearly four hundred. We pile up our chips and pass them in to the dealer. He hands out the greenbacks with a pleasant nod, which says "It is all right," and shove back from the table. In the forty-five minutes we sat there, three men were winners and seven were losers. The amount the three won is less than six hundred dollars, while the seven men have lost over four thousand! The bank is ahead. Our wine, supper, &c., is paid for. We have four odd checks —just enough to divide between the waiter who attended us at the table, the one who brought us cigars when we came in, the door-tender, and the boy in the coat-room.

It is nearly three o'clock; still the games go on. Here is a table where five men are playing poker for large stakes. Here sit two men and two of our handsome ladies at euchre, for fifty dollars a corner.

This is a gambling-house. It will be kept open till six in the morning. The crowd is not as when we entered. Some have gone home broke! Some have won enough to do them, and left. The balance are here. Some are in the little rooms about here, having a social chat over a glass of wine or a cigar. The ladies, who were so smiling five hours since, look war-worn and petulant. The waiters look somewhat sleepy. Still the game goes on. The dealer has been rested by his "partner," and another keen-eyed man draws the cards, takes, and pays. Men come here and lose in a night more than they made in a year. They use the funds of others.

If lucky, all is well; if unlucky, there is a bank defalcation, a deficit in some Government official's account, a breaking-up of some merchant, and no one stops to inquire into particulars.

"Are you going, gentlemen?"

"Yes; it's time countrymen were in bed, you know."

"Yes. Good thing! Take something before you go out? It's a raw night—must take care of health." And the polite proprietor insists on the acceptance of his hospitality.

We start for the door. A pretty *dame d'honneur*, with a smile and look of interest, invites us to call when convenient, wishes us good night, and smiles us into the hall—well satisfied that the Paris Club Rooms of New York are models of dissipation, ease, luxury, and extravagance. In the reception-room is a good fire. The ebony waiter carefully fixes on our overshoes, helps on our coat and furs, brushes our hat and overcoat, and bows his thanks as we give him a check. At the iron door stands the keeper of this institution. We drop a check into his hand; the doors open silently as before, and with a shiver we are outside, hastening into the carriage there in waiting, and down the almost deserted streets are rumbling along to our hotel, to sleep away the balance of the night, or morning, while our friends with us are satisfied with the adventures of the evening.

CHAPTER XIX.

MY FIRST NIGHT AT SPARKING.

WELL! She just took my eye—both eyes, for that matter! Young, gushing, bashful, laughing, happy black eyes, red cheeks, cherry lips, black hair, white teeth, voice like a warbler, laugh like the rising of a bride, step like a fawn, gait like a zephyr, heart like the noonday sun! Took my eye! Ay; she took my two eyes. Come to think of it, she took my heart along with my optics. She—God bless her animated photograph!—was just rising sixteen. Sweet? No name for it! I was older. I should be older, and I was. I was rising nineteen—hard on nineteen and a half.

We were neighbors. That is to say, our paternal relatives were neighbors, as the farms of our paternal relatives joined. My paternal relative was my uncle by birth, and I was his nephew; but the farms joined just the same as though nothing had happened. Her name was Eliza. Her name was a sweet name to me. It flowed into my heart so sweetly like, I rather liked it We met by chance—the usual way. I went to her house of an errand. She was there, and we met. I went for a pail of vinegar, and she poured it out for me. When I got home, my aunt said the vinegar wa'n't good. I knew why—Eliza had looked into its depths, and gave it sweetness!

She had a brother. He was older than either of us. Hank was his name, and he worked the farm. But I got to loving Eliza, if he did. We often met—in the orchard, when I went to steal fruit; and the old man—that is, her father—sent her to drive me out! Take care, old man! I am after t'other fruit what you hain't dreamed of!

It took her a good while to drive me out. I was often chased by her—chased so far I had to go part way home with her! Then, we met on the hills, when after berries.

> Lie still, fond heart;
> You're dreamin' on her now!

I used to show her the big bushes. I used to shove a handful of the ripe fruit into her basket, at times. This was before she was rising sixteen—at least two years before. When I first got to loving her, and she acted as if she knowed it, I used to pull the brush out of her path, and console her over the pricks and scratches she got from the thorny briars which beset our path.

Well! Time flew on, just as it always does. We increased in years, and I got to loving her more than a little. At last, I wanted to visit her by moonshine. It was in the fall of the season.

I had cut corn all day with my paternal uncle. I was tired; but love said to corn-cutting fatigue, "Get thee hence," and it henced to once.

I enveloped myself in a boiled shirt with linen collar. It was a turn-over collar. I put onto me a dickey belonging to my uncle. I had but few store-clothes of my own, as I was not wealthy in worldly dross and such! I put a couple squirts of mellow woodchuck-oil, scented with cinnamon-essence, on my hair. It smelt good—exceedingly good! I turned over a griddle on the stove, spit on its "contraband-colored" side, and with one end of an old clothes-brush polished my understanding. What a polish! It makes me sweat now, to think how I rubbed those faithful cowhide stogas! They were strong, if not graceful!

My paternal uncle and my other paternal aunt-cestor was in the other room. All this work I did in the kitchen. It was after seven o'clock in the evening. Gayly I sallied out of the wood-shed door, and with beating hopes wended my way down to the rustic brown farm mansion wherein dwelt Eliza.

It was a nice night—a very sweet, fragrant, moony night. A big time to make love to a girl rising sixteen! My heart was like a volcano all the way there. I went by the house—dasn't go in! Went down the road a few rods, and walked back by the gate. Saw her paternal relative sitting by the stove. Went past the gate again. Saw her other relative sitting by the table, darning. Went by the gate again—softly, so as not to waken the dog, as he and I were not very familiar. Saw Eliza at work by the stove, making cylindrical envelopes for sausages.

Went by again; fixed my hair, pulled down the lower end and pulled up the upper end of my shirt; turned, came back, and very carefully lifted the latch of the gate.

Not yet! My heart went like a carpet-whipper, and I walked off a little ways. Then I came back, got over the fence—kind of easy like—and waited. No one offered to hurt me, and the cinnamon stuff on my hair revived me. I went to the door. On it I knocked more than twenty knocks all at once.

"Deary me!" said the old lady.

"Some one at the door!" said the old man.

"And I at work in these ——!" said Eliza.

I waited a short, fleeting moment, and soon the old man came.

"Wy—how-de-deu, Brick?"—(only that wa'n't the name, then)—said he.

"Pretty well," said I.

"Are you?" said he.

"I am," said I.

"Did you knock?" said he.

"I did, indeed!" said I.

"I thought I heard you," said he

"0000000!" said I.

Then the old lady said, "Come in!" I then went in, and sat down. The old man—the sire

"Then she unhitched a little more toward the centre part of the store, and I hitched a little thus myself."—*See page* 170.

of the Eliza—then continued his avocation, which was a newspaper. Then the old lady, as she darned the stockings, conversed with me. She asked me how was my uncle—and my aunt —and me, myself—and the corn—and the apples —and the beef-cow—and the cider.

Then she took up to darn one of Eliza's stockings. She ran her hand into the extreme toe-end of it. How I wished it was my hand she was running into it! But it wa'n't!

Then she darned it, and asked me how was the bees—and the new fanning-mill—and the red steers—and the new well. She asked me lots of things, and I felt more calmer in my bosom.

Then Eliza came into my presence, and my heart went up again! Strange how she affected me inwardly, so! She took a seat and sat down.

I said nothing—only, "Good evening, 'Liza!" and I kinder laughed a little.

"Good evening!" said she, just as sweet!

Then the old man—her paternal—laid down

his paper, leaned forward, and put one hand on each knee. Then he looked at me and Eliza. Then he pulled off his boots, maintaining a severe silence meanwhile. Then he took off his stockings. Then he yawned, and said:

"Well, mother, guess I'll go to bed!" He then arose, went out on the door-step to see what kind of weather the morrow would bring forth, came in, and went to his couch!

Soon the maternal relative went to her retiracy, and we—that is, Eliza and I—were left alone.

This was the moment! On one side of the stove sat she; on the other side sat I. We thus sat some time. Then she hitched a little, and I unhitched a little. Then she unhitched a little more toward the centre part of the stove, and I hitched a little thus myself. Then she snugged toward me a little more! Then I rubbed my back against the chair, and I snugged toward her! Pretty soon "snugging" was played out, as we had reached.

* * * * * * *

We had not been so sweetly contagious to each other a bit more than two minutes by the old clock in the corner, when,

"'*Liza!*" came in sharp tones from the bedroom in which was the parents.

"Yes, mother!" said the fair and fragile daughter.

A moment or two with our hands close together.

"*Li-za! Remember that candles is candles!*"

"Yes, mother!" said the daughter, and she blew out the light.

"*Why, 'Liza!* how can 'Brick' see to get out?" came in wondering tones from the bedroom.

It was a hard job! We stumbled over the paternal's boots and over a chair, kissed the dear girl on the side of the head by mistake, and went home mad. On the way home, something said sparking wa'n't what it was cracked up to be; and a lacerated, crushed, and desponding heart indorsed the sentiment.

Two weeks after that I received a little piece of a shingle, on which was written in a neat hand, with red chalk:

"Eliza would be glad to have you call, Sunday night."

As my paternal uncle had no candles to spare, that I could take along, I didn't go; and she—poor girl!—was left.

Thus, like a wicked candle, my unwicked love was put out.

CHAPTER XX.

THE GIRLS.

TALK not to us of the city belle,
With her kangaroo stoop and Grecian swell,
But of—

THE GIRLS IN THE COUNTRY.

With lips that vie with the cherry,
Roguishness camped in their eyes—
With sleeves rolled up in the pantry,
Rolling away at the pies!
With a laugh like the sun in the morning,
Melting the hearts of their beaux!
Oh! the girls of the country forever—
The girls with cheeks like the rose!
Who can laugh—who can romp and be merry,
Whom you never can take by surprise!
Whom to meet it is dangerous, very:
For the heart stricken once by them dies,
Unless they will promise to marry!
And there's where the great trouble lies!

CHAPTER XXI.

STRUCK BY THE DIVINE AFFLATUS.

I WAS born about the first thing I can remember. It was so long ago it seems but yesterday, but it wa'n't. For several years I had no sweetheart, though my manly head was pillowed; but how, I will not tell. One day father brung home a bundle of stuff, with a smile hopping over his face like a one-legged tom-tit over an onion-bed. He said, "Make the boy some trousers, and see how he looks."

I heard it, and swelled up. My mother was a woman. If it hadn't been for her, I don't anticipate much. Mothers have much to do with good little boys. And the gentlemanly tailor who cut my legs to fit the trousers and sewed up the seams thereof, was a woman. This is why I took to them naturally. So affectionate was I for woman, that, if my father had hired a man, no matter how nice, for a wet-nurse, I do believe I'd have jumped the bounty, fled from the ramparts, forsook the fortifications, and dwelt with Solitude where are thy charms? One day a little boy came to our house visiting. That little boy wore a frock, and looked sort of funny to me. I showed him the grindstone, kittens, bee-hive, pigs, and all the little doings. Then I took him to the house. We were about eight years old apiece. The little boy was in bad humor, and cried. His mother, being sort of chivalrous, placed him on her two knees, and applied the flat of her hand—not to his head nor heels, nor to my head, but somewhere, and I believe I've forgotten. I witnessed the performance. This was my first knowledge of capital punishment.

Mother told me, when I asked her about it the next day, that the little boy was a girl, and I wondered if all girls were cross.

Then I forsook their company, and swore a life of celibacy. For years I was, so far as love was concerned, a hermit. My fancy fell on bread and butter with sugar onto it; mush and milk, with an occasional apple-dumpling. I roamed with the pigs, the cows, the horses, and the hens. I made voyages for eggs, and raised trouble with the cats who came with friendly intent to mow away the new-mown hay of their feline love. I was happy, except when compelled to ride a thin horse all day to plough corn, and no saddle. My soul soared above such doings, and my eager spirits chafed to be free, like the turkey pullet that bounds over the plain like a base-ball after chased grasshoppers.

And so sped me on to the terrors of a first mustache. Oh, mustache! I sing a pæan to thy glory now. The responsibilities thrust by experimenting Nature on my upper lip were of a harassing nature. But I lived to see that mustache sprout and come down, so to speak. Amid this glory, I blush to own the strength of my weakness.

Old Keyser lived two miles below our house. He was a shoemaker, and kept a peach-orchard. One day I wanted a waxed end to make a cracker for a whip. I went to his shoe-shop, and he said "Yea." Then I meandered into his orchard, and Congressionally appropriated a few of his best. He saw me, and advanced upon my unprotected rear with a raw-hide. I discovered his approach after my doom was sealed. I went to old Keyser's after a waxed end. Success came and dwelt with me. I got it—he gave it to me!

It is safe to say I was mad—moderately so, at least. I swore revenge. One night I went down to old Keyser's to rob his orchard. I wanted more of his fruit. I saw his daughter, Kuskurelia, and she sympathized with me. She gave me peaches, and told me to come often. She went a little way home with me. She was pretty. She was plump as a dumpling, and her lips seemed like two happy days telling pretty stories to each other.

When we parted, she handed me the last peach. It was luscious. We stood under a grape-vine by the road. As I took the peach, her forefinger and thumb touched mine. How my hand felt! It seemed as if nine hundred humming-birds had met in the palm of my hand to hold a sorosis meeting. I felt queer all over! Right back of my left ear I thought a full band was playing "Come where my Love lies dreaming."

May Mars forgive me, but I couldn't help it! I scorn to utter a lie. I am no politician, nor President. I can't lie, and, what is more, I won't. I dropped that peach, put one arm around her neck, one around her elbow, swooned down upon her lips like a twelve-pound baby in a new pillow just shook up.

Peaches never have been peaches since. Old Keyser's fruit was all a man could desire, and Kuskurelia was the bloomingest of all he possessed.

Memory doth not bring new-mown hay so sweet as that my first. And the way she put up her little lips! The moon saw it, and ran under a cloud. I have venerated moon ever since. I stood guard about those lips till the moon came out. Then we walked a little way up the road. Our pace was slower than the return of the Bull Run excursionists to Washington. Yes, indeed! Her hand was in mine. It seemed as if Cupid was ramming my left arm full of ten-thousand-pound cartridges, and forcing them into my heart a mile a second. My hair felt large and airy, like a bamboo fish-pole. Pretty soon we stopped by the corner of a fence. I slid my left arm around Kuskurelia's waist, dropped my right down on her left wrist and into her trembling palm; her head floated sidewise to my left shoulder-shift; my eyes went shut like an eclipse; her lips opened like an over-ripe nutmeg-melon; her breath came sweeter than the Songs of Solomon; there was a collision of two fond souls; Cupid moved in upon my heart as Forrest did at Fort Pillow, and I felt as if my backbone had been rented for an artillery-park, or Boston Peace Jubilee Coliseum.

Git eout! Move on! Don't stand on the corners! If you never went in love, do so quick. The little stars winked, as if they knew all about it. Nature sent about ninety-seven little breezes to fan our cheeks and flap the little wings of Cupid. Gently I sat Kuskurelia down on a rock, and twined myself confidingly close to her. We spoke of peaches, but there was no lustre in their stems. And the cool winds sighed about our flowing curls, till it seemed that the red head of Kuskurelia was a ten-mile torchlight procession leading a gallopade up and down the chambers of my heart. I was bewildered—at a loss for words. So I squoze her hand, and she squiz mine. Then I said, as on the dewy earth I lay with my head in her lap, my heels on a stump, and one of her lips just touching my forehead:

"Oh, Kuske, Kuske me ever!" And her eyes closed, and I felt as full of joy as a base drum full of Hail Columbia. And I said:

"Oh, Kuske, fruit of Keyser the venerable, peach of all peaches! you are the peach, and I am down! And here let us sweetly linger, while the moon goes cat-hopping from cloud to cloud, and all about us the zephyrs play like fingers in love's dalliance!" And she said:

"Brickey, dear, I don't mind the moon no more than the old man; but I've got to wash to-morrow. Let's go home."

So we arose, and returned with Kuskurelia to the domicile de Keyser. And there we lingered over lingerings in the lingerments of love, and again I tasted of that sweet bliss which springs from the divine afflatus, till she was ready to walk back with us. And so we walked all night. And from that day to this the taste of a peach has been full of strange melancholy, and the touch of a pretty girl's hand has consternated my existence; and the memory of that night with Kuskurelia lingers on the fond organ of my being like a wad of shoemaker's wax in your top-knot. But for the peaches, the Keyser, and his Kuskurelia, I had not been as I cannot hope to be again.

CHAPTER XXII.

AS A BASE BALLIST.

EUREKA!

Look at that brace of hands, once so soft and pretty, now suffused with the Egyptian blushes! Then look into those optics, and tell us tales of sympathy! And look at that Mount Tom on our right cheek-bone! Base ball! That is the row.

It came about thus: Secondary deployment is too shirksome for the system. The doctor said we needed exercise. Doctor knows. He told us to join base ball club. We joined. Bought a book of instructions, and for five days studied it wisely, if not too well. Then we bought a sugarscoop cap, a red belt, a green shirt, yellow trousers, punkin-colored shoes, a paper collar and purple neck-tie, and, with a lot of other delegates, moved gently to the grounds.

There were two nines. These nines were antagonists. The ball is a pretty little drop of softness the size of a goose-egg, and five degrees harder than a brick. The two nines play against each other. It is a quiet game, much like chess, only a little more *chase* than chess.

There was an umpire. His position is a hard one. He sits on a box and yells "Fowl!" His duty is severe.

I took the bat. It is a murderous plaything, descended from Pocahontas to the head of John Smith. The man in front of me was a pitcher He was *a nice* pitcher, but he sent the balls hot. The man behind me was a catcher. He caught it, too!

The umpire said, "Play!" It is the most radical play I know of, this base ball. Sawing cordwood is moonlight rambles beside base-ball. So the pitcher sent a ball toward me. It looked pretty coming, so I let it come. Then he sent another. I hit it with the club, and hove it gently upward. Then I started to walk to the first base. The ball lit in the pitcher, or his hands, and somebody said he caught a fly. Alas, poor fly! I walked leisurely toward the base. Another man took the bat. I turned to see how he was making it, and a mule kicked me on the cheek. The man said it was the ball. It felt like mule, and I reposed on the grass. The ball went on!

Pretty soon there were two more flies, and three of us flew out. Then the other nine came in, and we nine went out. This was better. Just as I was standing on my dignity in the left field, a hot ball, as they called it, came sky-rocketing toward me. My captain yelled, "Take it!"

I hastened gently forward to where the ball

was aiming to descend. I have a good eye to measure distances, and saw at a glance where the little aerolite was to light. I put up my hands. How sweetly the ball descended! Everybody looked. I felt something warm in my eye. "Muffin!" yelled ninety fellers. "Muffin, be d——! It's a cannon-ball!" For three days I've had two pounds of raw beef on that eye, and yet it paineth!

Then I wanted to go home, but my gentle captain said "Nay." So I nayed, and stayed. Pretty soon it was my strike. "Brick to bat!" yelled the umpire. I went, but not all serene, as was my wont. The pitcher sent in one hip-high. I missed it. He sent in another neck-high. It struck me in the gullet. "Fowl!" yelled the umpire. He sent in the ball again. This time I took it square, and sent it down the right field, through a parlor window, a kerosene lamp, and rip up against the head of an infant who was quietly taking its——nap in its mother's arms.

Then I slung the bat, and meandered forth to the first base. I heard high words, and looked. When I slung the bat, I had with it broken the jaw of the umpire, and was fined ten cents.

The game went on. I liked it. It is so much fun to run from base to base just in time to be put out, or to chase a ball three-fourths of a mile down-hill, while all the spectators yell "Muffin!" "Go it!"—"Home run!"—"Go round again!" —or, "Go round a dozen times!" Base-ball is a sweet little game. When it came my turn to bat again, I noticed everybody moved back about ten rods! The new umpire retreated twelve rods. He was timid! The pitcher sent 'em in hot. Hot balls in time of war are good;—but I don't like 'em too hot for fun. After a while I got a fair clip at it, and you bet it went! cutting the daisies down the right field. A fat man and his dog sat in the shade of an oak, enjoying the game. The ball broke one leg of the dog, and landed like a runaway engine in the corporosity of the fat man. He was taken home to die.

Then I went on a double-quick to the field, and tried to stop a hot ball. It came towards me from the bat at the rate of nine miles a minute. I put up my hands. The ball went sweetly singing on its way, with all the skin from my palms with it.

More raw beef!

That was an eventful chap who first invented base ball.

It's such fun! I've played five games, and this is the glowing result:

Twenty-seven dollars paid out for damages.

One bunged eye, badly bunged.

One broken little finger.

One bump on the head.

Nineteen lame backs.

A sore jaw.

One thumb dislocated.

Three sprained ankles.

Five swelled legs.

One dislocated shoulder, from trying to throw a ball a thousand yards.

Two hands raw from trying to stop hot balls.

A welt the size of a hornet's-nest on my left hip, well back.

A nose sweetly jammed; and five uniforms spoiled from rolling in the dirt at the bases.

I have played two weeks, and don't think I like the game. There is not a square inch on, in, or under me, but aches. I sleep nights dreaming of hot balls, "flys," "*fouls*," and descending "sky-rockets."

But I am proud of my proficiency in the game. It's fine exercise—a little easier than being run through a threshing machine, and not much, either. It's a nice game for a poet or orator; 'twill make one *sore* beyond all accounts.

I've looked over the scorer's book, and find that in two weeks I've broken seven bats, made one tally, broken one umpire's jaw, broken ten windows in adjoining houses, killed a baby, broke the leg of a dog and mortally injured the bread-basket of a spectator, knocked five other players out of time by slinging my bat, and knocked the waterfall from a school-marm who was standing twenty rods from the field, a quiet looker-on.

I've used up fifteen bottles of arnica liniment, five bottles of lotions, half a raw beef, and am so full of pain that it seems as if my bones were but broken bats, and my legs the limbs of a dead horse-chestnut, instead of the once elastic trotters of Thine,

"B." P.

CHAPTER XXIII.

THE TOILER BY THE SEA.

Gay as a waterfall—
Indeed were she!
Her pap was a deacon
In Marble-h-e-a-D!

WHERE the high-rolling billows kissed the feet of the shore and wet the stones on the beach, on the periphery of that Christianized land known as New England, lived a toiler by the sea. He was a Puritan delegate of high renown, and made his living by deaconizing in a Marblehead church, building fires on a high rock, and gathering up the little things washed ashore from the vessels wrecked by the poor captains who made for his false light, thinking it to be a regular light-house.

He was a kind-hearted thief as ever robbed a corpse, and was so interested in temperance, that he poured barrels of rum down his New England gullet to keep visitors from igniting themselves thereby! He revelled in a red house, carried the key to the church, rejoiced in the Scripture name of Ananias, and was weaned on paregoric; else he had not put his family to sleep nights, so long and loud were his prayers. His t'other name was Jimplecute, and he was in all respects Ananias Jimplecute.

Once, when I was a young lad, striving with a pair of straps on the lower end of my pants, manfully struggling with an incipient mustache, and rejoicing in the elegant manner in which I could write my name on a school-house door with a piece of charcoal, I meandered by the home-temple of A. J., and looked in.

The eminent New England Christian was a rooster that crowed loud. It was a calm, still night. There was no storm raging to drive ships out of their track. The moon was doing her best; and A. J. was, as I was gliding past his door, on the devotion much. He was always thus when there were no wrecks on the coast. He had a daughter! She was a female—bound in health, and of much muscle, so-called. She knelt in the open door on a calm summer eve, her bare feet pointing to a pan of dough on the hearth, in which were reposing a litter of young kittens—to make them docile, I presume!—her face looking toward the silent roar of the distant waves, while with a fish-spear she was digesting the devotion of her paternal, and gently scratching the back of a swine, which lay like a ship in the trough of a mud-hole near the door. The touching beauty of the scene filled me with novel awe. I blew my nose, and gently lingered.

The daughter's name was Tibelius. And this

was the prayer she was listening to! I winked majestically at Tibelius, and drew nigh. Her paternal had been engaged a full hour when I arrove. He had visited the heathen of the distant lands, and was gently on his way home. And thus prayed he:

"And now, Lord of love and peace, wilt Thou not confuse Thine enemies, and bow the necks of all who live in wealth and pride, and are far removed from Marblehead and Thee! Let the heathen rage, and protect me and mine. Look down upon the African and Africaness, that they may be happy, as we are happy! Give fur shirts to the Tim-buc-tos and fans to the Rus-si-ans, for they know not what they do. And teach all men to love Thee as I do. And give us prosperity, peace, and good-will, and confuse all other churches but the one in Marblehead; and prosper that, for I wish to sell it a building-lot. And hold the ships on the sea in the hollow of Thy hand, and from distant lands send them swiftly to New England. And then, let sickness spare those whose wages are paid in advance; and in storms direct the eyes of the captains, not toward the steady light in the harbor, but to the higher light I have erected on Round Rock summit, that the ships that contain valuable goods may be dashed to pieces on the beach beneath, as a warning to those who would seek to become rich, and that I may be busy—for the devil loves an idle man. And spare Thou the poor sailors everywhere; but if they are wrecked, let them die quickly before they reach the shore, so I shall not be obliged to bury them, except they have valuables in their pockets! *Amen!* Old woman, wind the clock!"

How I loved that man—that true New England Christian! He was such a good man! He had such a heart for those who suffered! I venerated his tallowed hair. And I loved the fair two-hundred cherub who winked at me innocently with the spear in one hand. Ananias was a tender-hearted man. He used to send his daughter out to kindle a fire on the rock when the storm was howling. And the next day, when the beach would be strewn with spoons, watches, pianos, books, furniture, bales of cotton, Bibles, mules, and wounded men who had been driven ashore on an inhospitable coast by following the light there kindled to blind them, with what tenderness would he move around among them! How sweetly he would gather up their valuables and tote them to a place of safety! And he would so kindly drop a box, or an anvil, or a chunk of iron, on the heads of the wounded ones, to put them out of misery! He was very kind! He carried strychnine to give those in agony, and removed their money and jewelry in order to prepare their souls for heaven! And to each one he thus relieved he would give a tract, or have Tibelius sit by their side and read the sermon of Christ on the Mount. It looked so sweet to see that good saint of Marblehead bearing the burdens of the day, growing crooked under the loads of plunder he carried away to remove all thoughts of wealth from the hearts of the poor ones he was caring for so kindly! And it looked like the tint of August, to see that dear girl of Ananias, clad in the dresses, laces, jewelry, and pretty things once worn by the wives and sisters of the poor wrecked ones, to remind them, in their dying hours, of

Home, sweet home!
There is no place like home!

as she would sit there and read to them from her little tracts, and try so hard to turn their thoughts heavenward! And when they wanted to give thanks to A. J. and his daughter, how tenderly would A. J. and those under him hold their hands over the mouths of those who would speak —lest talking weary them, you know! And how touching it was to see the wrecked ones doing as they were bid!—to see them roll over and fill their mouths with wool, and smile on the angel of peace born from the loins of that New England Christian, without a murmur! And to see the young men of the prairie, back of Marblehead, lugging plunder continually to enrich the New England Puritan; working, toiling unceasingly, uncomplainingly, helping bury the wrecked ones as fast as A. J. should drop items of weight on their heads to gently cease their misery.

CHAPTER XXIV.

KISSING IN DREAMS.

ON my bed in slumber sweet
  I revelled in Dreams of love.
'Twas the noon of night—the silent street
  Was still as the starry hosts above.
I sweetly dreamed that my strong arm
  Was round her neck so white and dear—
That she sought me out, and safe from harm,
  With kisses told she knew no fear.

I gently drew her to my breast
  And kissed and kissed her lips so free,
And she kissed back, and there at rest
  In dreams how happy then were we!
At last this kissing woke me up,
  And there, his face close to my head,
Lay Victor, my young pointer pup,
  Who in dead of night had found my bed!

CHAPTER XXV.

LAKE ROSS SEWING-CIRCLE.

"Alas! and did my Saviour bleed
For such a worm as I?"

BRIDGET, put the breakfast-dishes to soak, and cut a lunch for my dear husband! Sweep the cobwebs out of the best room, and open the window there, so it won't smell so close. Then mop the floors, empty the old left dishes in the pantry, scour the knives on that new bath-brick, run over to Mrs. Buzzy's and borrow her tea-spoons and a double drawin' of tea, take the young ones over to Aunt Hanner's, so they won't squall, borrow a clean table-cloth of Mrs. Haran, and get ready for the Sewing Society this afternoon; while I go and learn a few verses of the Bible, and a little snatch of three or four hymns to repeat and sing; for you know I am an officer of the Sewing Society, and, as it meets here to-day, I must appear rather smart. And the minister is coming to tea; so you must borrow an extra spoon of somebody."

"Yes'm!"

Mrs. Talky was a nice, pious sister of one of the Lake Ross churches. She had long been a lively ant in the Christian sugar-bowl; and, as she had the longest tongue of any sister of the flock, she could out-talk the others, and thus ranked high. That afternoon the Sewing Society met at her house to make pin-cushions for the nigger babies down South, and to ku-klux the reputations of those who did not belong to the Society.

Bridget went hence to arrange for the festive ceremonies, Mrs. Talky learned her lessons, and two o'clock found the dirt swept well behind the doors and under the bed—for Mrs. Talky was a marvel of neatness—and all in readiness, except the tea.

At three o'clock the female panorama of Samaritanism had gathered in Mrs. Talky's parlor, each with her work. It promised to be a big day for the down-trodden wards of the nation.

Mrs. Talky was high wren of the cage. Mrs. Waggle, a demure little lady of one baby and prospects, was Secretary, and a vigilant worker on a lamp-mat for a nigger church. Mrs. Squawk, a long-nosed sister, who knew much and wanted to know more, was building a slipper-pattern for Fred. Douglass.

Mrs. Noall, a blooming widow of fifty, who knew more than the law allowed of sinful natures in general, was President, and did nothing.

There were twenty-one ladies present, and much good was accomplished.

At half-past three the labor of the day was

finished, when the real object of the meeting broke out.

Mrs. Noall was folding up the work, when an allusion was made to Mr. Marm, one of her neighbors.

"Oh, that horrid Marm!" said Mrs. Noall. "I know him. I knew him years ago. I have long been intimately acquainted with him, and he is the worst man but ten in Lake Ross."

Here the conversation became general, and all the sisters took a shot at the bird on the wing.

"That is so! I know all about his doings."

"And that poor wife of his'n! She actually mends his pants! And they do say they use butter only once a day!"

"Good enough for her! She knew what he was when she married him."

"I saw him talking to Miss Jones, the other day, and he never seemed to care a bit when I caught him at it!"

"Just like all the men!"

"Except mine!"

"Except mine!"

"And mine!"

"Well, I don't care for Marm; but do you know how Brown acts, Mrs. Talky, when he goes in company?"

"I should say so, love! But they do say he drinks terribly! He drinks so bad, and is so jealous, that his wife—poor woman!—has to let the Doctor in the back way, nights, to see him, when he is asleep. She thinks so much of him!"

"Of who?"

"Her husband, of course!"

"Pshaw! I know better. No woman can love a man who won't buy her more than four new bonnets a year! That is impossible!"

"Did you see Miss Smith's bonnet, to-day? *Such* a gawk! And old Smith is rich, but awful stingy! Won't his children be glad when he dies!"

"Well, his money ain't his'n. It don't belong to him; it's mortgaged."

"Oh! did you know that Mrs. Black had a baby?"

"No!"

"Do tell!"

"Yes; it was born to-day, and weighs ten pounds. It is a boy. I went over to borrow a churn, and asked. And I wanted to see if Mrs. Black had a new carpet. Mrs. White said she had."

"Mrs. White! *Pshaw!* The proud thing! Because she keeps a horse and *two* hired girls, she needn't stick up her nose above other people! I know when she hadn't a sh—illing to her back! And she never would have been anybody, if she hadn't married young White, who had money. They say she *had* to marry him! You know, their first child wa'n't born till the second winter —and that proves all I've said."

"Oh, that's nothing to Miss Green! You know what she did?"

"Yes; and the more shame for her, to get their minister in such a scrape! Ministers is human, as we all are; and I never blame 'em when they come around me."

"Well, what do you think of Rev. Mr. Stone? He goes to see Deacon Wood's wife every day. She wants too much praying to suit me! They say he goes to give music-lessons on the melodeon; but I don't believe a word of it."

"I don't see what there is so attractive about her! I thought he had better taste!"

"She acts like Mrs. Jones, who always sticks her nose up when she comes in church. We wouldn't have her there, but her husband has got money, and pays."

"Have you heard about Miss Twig?"

"La, no! What is it?"

"Ah, it is such a shame, I blush to tell it! You know, she was to be married to young

Beans. Well, she was sick, last week. Mrs. Wiggle's hired girl told my hired girl that Mrs. Naggle's hired girl told her that she heard the doctor say that she had been eating too much succotash? That's Beans! The Doctor needn't try to lie out of it!"

"Mebbe he will marry that Miss Dix he used to go with!"

"I don't believe it! She has no taste in dress. And she is so nasty about the house! The last time I was there she actually blacked the cook-stove with a rag!"

"Her father ought to be ashamed of himself!"

"Did you hear about Deacon Jenks?"

"No. What is it?"

"Why, I thought everybody knew it! You know, he hired Matilda Miggles to wash for him a year. When his wife died, he said he wanted Matilda to take care of the children. One night, as I was passing the house, I peeked in the kitchen-window, and saw Matilda go into the parlor where the Deacon was sitting, and shut the door. I know a thing or two! Now, the Deacon has gone to a water-cure with his children, and taken Matilda along! I know what is what!"

"Can it be possible!"

"Do tell!"

"Well, I never!"

"I can't believe it!"

"Nor I. But you know that the Deacon had that reputation before he joined the church."

"I wonder why Mrs. Judd don't join the church?"

"Oh, her husband has failed, and can't buy a pew."

"Good enough for them! I sha'n't visit *them* any more!"

"Well, I wonder if Bill Birch and Carrie Colton ever intend to get married?"

"I don't believe they do. Bill is tough. He laughs at our minister, and says we are a lot of

"Here comes the minister! Oh, he is such a dear, good man! and he has his pockets full of newspapers."—*See page* 209.

old hens! and I have told Carrie not to marry him."

"Well, what does he go to see Mrs. Wriggle for? He professes to be such a friend of the family, and always spends his evenings there! That means something!"

"Of course it does!"

"Well, I never heard of it!"

"It's so, and I don't care who knows it!"

"There goes Mrs. Ochre! What horrid tassels!—her old dress made over into a walking one."

"How I hate such snobbery!"

"And I!"

"Well, that is all you can expect of her—of any one who belongs to that church!"

"That's so!"

"Well, that church ain't so nice as ours will be!"

"Here comes the minister! Oh, he is such a dear, good man!—and he has his pockets full of newspapers."

We saw the party seated at supper, admiring the conquered spoons, borrowed from a returned chaplain, and could not help thinking that the Lake Ross Sewing Society was a big thing!

CHAPTER XXVI.

PRETTY WAITER-GIRL SALOONS.

AT six o'clock we dine at a hotel or boarding-house, and consider the work of the day, especially for business men and strangers, well-nigh done. As New York is a great city in every sense of the word, it is worth while to see and know of its peculiar institutions.

The waiter hands our overcoat and overshoes. Turn the fur collar well about the ears, for the night is very cold. Out from the warm hotel into the bitter air. The walks are covered with pedestrians hurrying by.

"Some in rags,
Some in jags,
And some in velvet gowns."—

borrowing a snatch from an old song. The drivers on the omnibuses sit wrapped like doll-babies going visiting, and, with head drawn in like a turtle, guide their tired horses and loads of freezing passengers through the equine sea and mass of carriages. Here and there is a cart; here and there a horse down on the smooth, cold, hard, stone-covered street, lying quiet and stunned, or plunging wildly to regain a treacherous foothold.

Never mind the omnibuses, nor stop to look or sympathize with fallen horses; for fallen humanity is more of a study. Up Broadway, past the stores closed for the night—by the tempting show-windows of retail dealers in useful and fancy articles—past the marble-fronted hotels—by the variegated gas-light signs and large lamps indicating places of amusement—and still on up the wonderful street.

Down there is a large oyster-cellar, where a thousand men per day tempt and satisfy their palates with fat bivalves. Down there is a mammoth restaurant or dining-saloon, where citizens and strangers supply the inner man with food and beverage, and where "single gentlemen with their wives," in cozy little rooms looked in upon but by God and a close-mouthed waiter, drink their wine, eat game suppers, and prepare the way for misery. Hell has many "improvement companies" in New York, and secures volunteers without recourse to a draft other than that of the son of Jupiter and Semele.

Blaze and glitter, gas-light and tinsel! Now we come to underground saloons, where the transparencies on the walk inform us that Miss Frank, or Miss Nellie, or Miss Kate, has a Concert-Saloon. The sign says music and dancing are free. It says the prettiest waiter-girls in the city are there.

"Let us go down."

No; not now. The finest are not on Broadway, and we will reserve an inspection of these till we have looked in upon those of a better class—if better there be to these dormer-windows of damnation.

To the left. Do not hurry, for there is plenty of time. Eight o'clock is but the preface of the evening. Never mind who these are we are meeting and passing continually. Only waiting—nothing more! Across Mercer street, once so famous, or infamous, and still more than a ghost of its ugliness. Here is Greene street. To the left. Here comes a horse-car—red light; fare six cents. We go to the right. Never mind, driver; we'll jump on. Sit close, for the car is crowded; but look out for jams, for such things are severe on watches and pocket-books.

Some way out of the business-part of town we

are going. It would be a long walk from the sleeping dead who rest 'neath the ancient gravestones bordering lower Broadway, north side—a long distance from the tower of Trinity—nearer the brown-stone fronts of ease, fashion, and luxury—we dare not say comfort and contented happiness.

The pretty waiter-girl saloon is an institution of magnitude in this city. By actual count of police officers, it is known that the number of such saloons in New York is two hundred and twenty-three; while the number of girls—of course, all are pretty—is nearly two thousand.

The one we are going to is the most fashionable in New York. It is on that aristocratic line of travel known as Fifth avenue, and is entered on three streets.

Down the broad and well-lighted stairs. No danger of slipping, for the steps are kept cleaner than at the churches. Silently the door opens as we touch the knob—opened by a male waiter inside. What a glare of light! How warm and comfortable! One hundred and sixty feet in width, two hundred and thirty feet deep, is this palace of dissipation. The floors are of variegated marble, cut in diamond-surfaced blocks, and matched with all an artist's care. Here are billiard-tables a half dozen, but the players are few. Here are little round marble tables, where men sit playing draughts or dominos. Through the centre length of the room runs an opened wall. We look through the openings, and see, to the right, a crowd. Here are about sixty tables, and about forty pretty waiter-girls, so-called. The room is kept to a comfortable heat, while an air of languor pervades the apartment. We sit down—four of us—by a round table, first carelessly nodding to a girl sauntering near. She joins our party. Would you see her?

Look, then. She is not yet twenty years of age, but is educated in full. She knows at a glance whether you are from the country—

whether a man who has travelled—whether a sport, or business man residing in the city—and acts accordingly. She is good-looking, except that the wanton is lurking deep in her eyes. And in the matter of dress, no lady in the land excels her. Rustling silk, with amplitude of crinoline; her waist looks all that artist could wish; her hair is dressed to the apex of fashion; her fingers are covered with rings, and her person generally well ornamented. In the country she would captivate deacons, merchants, business men, and perhaps editors, were they easily caught.

She sits easily down, with a pleasant, smiling "Good-evening, gentlemen." She addresses you by some familiar name, as "Little one," "General," "Deacon," or "Darling," as she judges will best please. On her breast is a number—each girl is given a number-badge, as they come in at seven o'clock to enter upon the work of the evening. By these numbers their accounts are kept at the bar. We order drinks for the party—of course inviting one or more girls to join, as their looks strike the fancy. We pay large prices for all sorts of villanous compounds; and, of course, our pretty waiter drinks with us. It may be that she takes a hot lemonade, a brandy punch, a gin cocktail, whiskey straight, port julep, hot whiskey, or glass of ale, as her taste calls for. She trips off to the bar—gives her orders. The glasses are set out to her. She gives from a pocketful of checks, which in the hands of the barkeeper are debit against her, and trips smilingly back with the fluid. She seats herself beside us. The glasses jingle—sides, "tops and bottoms," or table knocks—and we drink. Then comes a chat. Generally the girl gets the odd change. She gently lays her hand on your arm to whisper something, or to ask a question. Her soft hand plays with yours on the sly. She pulls imaginary splinters or chips of tooth-picks from your whiskers, and "purrs" like a love-asking kitten. She is so affectionate, one cannot help feeling an interest in her. We ask, and she tells her history, as we sit a little apart from the rest. Hugo's fiction excelled! "She is a young widow—poor, but honest parents. Husband killed in the army. Is forced to do this, or starve. She earns six dollars a week, and five per cent. on all nightly sales over twenty dollars." You wonder how she dresses so well on six dollars a week, when it costs nine for board! Overchange sometimes, when gentlemen treat! And the proprietor thinks much of her, and pays *her* extra wages! Or she is a young girl just from the country. Or she is a milliner, and her shop is busted, and she does this for a living. Of course, she is strictly virtuous. Yet—if there ever was a man—you, who so resemble a dear friend somewhere, might be just the man—if—and if—and if—oh, dear! And we all drink again.

There are as many different styles of pretty

girls here as there are waiters. Here is a queen of night—eyes and hair of raven blackness, dressed like a queen, beautiful and enticing. Beware there, countryman! She is more beautiful than the woman you love, perhaps; but never mind. Another comes, dressed in mourning. She has just lost a mother (or something else), and tells you a sorrowful tale, and, half-weeping, says Yes to any proposition, except to edit a daily paper! And here comes a red-cheeked girl, dressed so prettily, with a natural rose in her hair—no jewelry, no display—that even a city sport is tempted to fall in love with the little minx.

The saloon is filled with pretty girls, who are here from seven to half-past one every night. After the latter hour, time is their own.

The saloon is fitted up regardless of cost. Marble tables—marble counters—full-length mirrors—easy-chairs—brilliant lights—a large fountain playing into a marble basin six feet across, filled with gold-fish—canary birds hanging in the evergreen branches, which form little screens or bowers in the corners of the room, or by some pillar where sits a gray-haired sinner, half-hidden from gaze of curious eyes, holding the hand of a pretty waiter-girl, who has him on a string, for sure! In one corner of the room a piano sits, and at intervals a Polish, Hungarian, or German "professor" favors us with operatic or other airs.

The room is warm—the blood gets hot—the pretty waiter-girls grow sociable as the small hours draw nigh. There is nothing to offend the most polite. Loud talking, profanity, and unseemly conduct is not allowed. A police officer is always in the room, to preserve order and eject those who are too noisy. The proprietor walks about, seeing that all is well. The hours fly past. It is cold outside—comfortable here. We play a game of dominos, to see who pays the next drinks. Our girl trips off for a minute, to wait on somebody else. She returns smilingly, just as the game is finished, ready for another chat. She tells all her little troubles, and the history of every girl she dislikes who is present; for pretty waiter-girls have their jealousies as well as other people. If you order drinks from another girl, she does not like it. She tells you her name, which is Anna, Emma, Katie, Frank, Belle, Sophia, Alice, Nellie, Carrie, or some such pet name. She invites you—that is, if she likes your style—to call at such a number on such a street, and visit—just for acquaintance' sake, you know! Or, perhaps you would as soon walk or ride home with her when the saloon closes. Saloons *do* close in New York!

Being a stranger, with nothing to do, of course you would not object to going just a little way with a pretty girl, to protect her from loafers, you know!

These girls have their regular customers, whose patronage is their capital. We have seen them go half-crazy with anger, when some regular evening dropper-in at the saloon would give an order to some other girl who had never before waited on him. They fix up a man's coat-collar to keep his ears warm, go with him to the door, and say, "Come again!—Call for 'Frank,' or 'Kate!'—Good-night!" with such a winning way, that a man thinks pretty waiter-girls and pretty waiter-girl saloons are great institutions.

As a general thing, these girls are sharp. They know who to spend time talking with, and who not to. It is not every one they will waste words with, of all the hundreds who nightly visit this place in particular.

They are the Grisettes and Lorettes of Paris, only sharper and more mercenary.

Most of the patrons of these institutions are strangers, and, of course, better paying customers than residents of the city. Men come and go. They become interested in the girls. They bring friends to these saloons, and swell the receipts to sums ranging from one to three hundred dollars a night. You get anything, from wine to ice-water, from a raw oyster to a cold turkey—of course paying well for it.

At half-past one the hour for closing arrives. The crowd is thinned down to but few more than there are girls. One by one or two by two they go mated, if not matched. The saloon is still—the customers have taken their last drink—the girls have put on their things and gone, with or without an escort, as they were enticing or in luck—the police officer goes home—the bar-tenders take a "night-cap" drink—the cashier and proprietor figure up the receipts and lock up the cash—the girls' number-badges are strung ready for to-morrow night—first come, first numbered—the gas is turned down—the porter locks the doors and goes off to his room, perhaps a mile or more away—and the pretty waiter-girl saloon is closed till to-morrow night at seven o'clock, when all is light and "splendor" again.

The influences of these saloons are evil—only

evil continually. Men come here singly and in groups—many but to see and extend their knowledge of human nature. Some come to drink; some to chat with the girls, who are always striving to please, and who have their friends and admirers, whose coming is looked for each night. Men come here because they have the blues—to see the girls, and watch others. They come and buy a drink—anything from lemonade to hot poison—or take a cold lunch, look about, and go home.

The girls are generally all one thinks them to be. They receive low wages, but live by picking up flats. Clerks in stores, business men, strangers, and others, fall in love—what an insult to the word!—make them presents, buy their smiles and favors, and, strange as it may seem, at times marry the inmates of these legalized concerns. They are of the selectness which sends disease far over the land, and would be abolished but for the influence they wield at the polls. The votes of the Five Points, and such localities, are in a manner counteracted by the "aristocracy" of politics which run the votes which cluster around such places.

CHAPTER XXVII.

TO A PRETTY LITTLE MAID.

MY pretty little maid
Whose gentle heart for love is yearning,
Better be a wee afraid —
And closer watch the coals a-burning!
Lovers talk of joy and sorrow,
True to-night — and false to-morrow.
Boys will talk of earnest loving.
Men will dally in their roving.
Some for one thing — some another,
— Wed the one and love the other!
My pretty little maid,
Don't sit there listening
When up and off to bed
You had better be hastening!

My pretty little maid,
Don't believe all the praising —
All the words so smoothly said
Till you've learned your lover's raising!

Men will talk, ne'er believing,
Happy when you maids deceiving.
    Men will vow, and then forgetting
    Leave you to your vain regretting,
Twenty court for your undoing—
One is earnest in his wooing.
    Darling little maid,
        You'd better be hastening
    Away to your bed,
        And not there be listening!

CHAPTER XXVIII.

PURIVILLE BENEVOLENCE.

WE had a high old time in Puritanville, or Puriville, as we call it. The winter's snows all ran down the creek. Our New England hills sang with joy as the ice ripped and the water rippled on its grapevine-way to the deep blue sea.

In all our settlement lives not a single, married, or double Democrat. We are all loyal in Puriville—and refined—and so Christian-like in disposition! We never jerk the last egg from the nest—till the active pullet has tired of her eggs-periments, and gives up her eggs-ultation over our eggs-centricity of taking all we get, except the shells!

Every Sunday our dear, pious divine, Rev. Hezerky Dropchin, preaches such soothing sermons at us! He tells us that h-e and two ells is paved ninety feet deep with skulls of infants cemented in with the curses of the d-a-m-ned ones—and that the Lord loveth a cheerful giver—and that giving to the poor is investing with the Lord. And he says we must love our enemies—or we can't make a cent out of seventeen of them.

He is a good man, is Rev. Hezerky Dropchin, and preaches with most unctuous *éclat.* And we do just as he tells us to; for why doctor yourself, when you buy his doctorin's?

One day, while the sprouts were sprouting, the buds were budding, the leaves leaving, and the grass grassing all over things generally, the bell rang a loud Christian-like rangle, calling us all to worship. Ours is a nice bell—it was conquered from a church-tower when our troops were on their Southern "tower," and now rings "Glory hallelujah" in the hands of a Northern jerkist. It is wicked to be proud, and God loves us in Puriville for confiscating all such articles of "bigotry and virtue" from the South, and reconstructing them *Via* the plan of roundhead salvation. And we have such nice carpets, and hymn-books, and a Bible, and that aristocratic solid silver communion service, all taken from the proud people of the South, who would have ended their days in much continuous torment had we not taken their idols from them, and directed their eyes to the true and revealed Power.

It is so sweet to save souls this way. And it's cheaper for us. And then, our churches will seem *so* homelike when visiting brethren and sisters visit us in our own prayer-warmed homes, to attend divine service with us!

The other day Brother Dropchin told us that

his dear cousin 'Zekiel had been South. And such destitution he never saw. He went down with two thousand cheap pictures to sell to the innocent contrabandboxes of the South, but they had been supplied, and he only sold seven damaged "views" in all his trip! And he had two thousand dollars' worth of brass jewelry, but the white men of the South had so outraged, robbed, and impoverished the negroes, that they—poor innocent architects of national cemeteries!—had no spelter to shell out; and so his jewelry gangrened, and he returned with it in verdigris.

Then, after a prayer and two songs, our beloved pastor said we must do something for the poor people of the South, to let them know that we forgave them for their wickedness, and to win them back to a love for their benefactors. He said they needed school-books, and old clothes, and reading-matter, and money, and encouragement.

We all felt it our duty to aid in restoring these

poor disfreckled sinners to their rights and religion. So we appointed a committee to solicit aid for the poor half-whipped rebels, that they might know we love them. And everybody responded. Our people are *so* liberal! Indeed, God loves a cheerful giver; and if the folks South do not love us, it ain't our fault. We give them good advice, and good laws, to match the articles sent to them by our committee, C. O. D.!

Our committee did first-rate. In two days we raised twelve big boxesful of things for them, and sent them off. Deacon Gunner had them stored in his barn, four miles from the depot, and his son John hauled them to the cars for four dollars a box, advance charges paid, and forwarded for collection!

Then we had them repacked in new boxes—thirty-seven dollars, advance charges, forwarded for collection. And they all went on *via* Oswego, Cape May, St. Paul, La Crosse, Pittsburg, to St. Louis; thence by ocean steamer to New

Orleans, and up the river to Morrison, Illinois, and then by cars direct to the South.

There were lots of things in the boxes the people of the South need. In one box were:

Seventeen pairs of old, moldy boots, of 1818—good as new.

Twenty old hoop-skirts taken from the lanes and streets.

One waterproof night-cap, ruffled on the back.

Two old boot-jacks, split.

Nine straw hats, averaging forty-one years old, selected from the cock-loft over the wagon houses.

Another hoop-skirt—boy's size. Two umbrella covers, perforated. One claw-hammer, without teeth. Two dozen tracts on the Incalculable Horrors of Perpetual Damnation. One tin horn run over by a cart laden with stone.

Twelve pill-boxes to hold garden-seeds. One red overcoat, without a tail. Two dozen shirts, assorted sizes, minus flaps, arms, bosoms, buttons, or other wrinkles.

Three pairs of second-hand stove-legs, good as new.

Likeness of a bob-tailed cat—good to amuse Sunday-school children. One pair of curling-tongs, bent, and only a little rusty.

Two dozen of them things you buy in pairs at a store, providing you need them.

One flannel shirt for the baby to wear, in the sweet summer-time.

One lot of carpet-bags, and loyal sneak-thieves to carry them.

One dozen old socks, scalloped and assorted.

One copy of a cook-book to stay their appetites.

The other boxes were filled with like goods. And, now that we have done our duty, and shown to the people of the South how much we love them, we are happy and contented.

CHAPTER XXIX.

WHAT I KNOW ABOUT FARMING.

I AM a pharmer. One of the olden kind! About ninety-five year olden kind. When younger than now, I had much to do with Weeds! This fact makes me a pharmer. There is nothing about the science of pharming, from sitting of a hot day under a rail-fence in company with a jug, to picking geese, that I do not feel justified in knowing. Picking geese is good. I have helped pluck many a goose—from the black Michi-ganders to the last Republican candidate for Governor in the State of New York.

Observe the following rules about pharming

the result of sixty years' subsoil ploughing to find the floor of the philosopher's office. These instructions, if not right, are according to copy-right, and will be useful to office-clerks, octogenarians, and those who raise bees on a pole; also to the poor of large cities, who should borrow a few thousand dollars of their friends, go West, settle alongside of some railroad where the land has been properly Grant-ed to men who are willing to sell what cost them nothing, for fifty dollars an acre, including back taxes.

In selecting land, great care should be taken to get bottom-lands—that is, lands with a bcttom to them. It is just as easy to enter them, without the danger of going clear through. Hill-lands are apt to make pharming a one-sided affair, the price paid for such property, as a genoral thing, being a little steep.

Stones and stumps are not essential to good farms, unless you have plenty of dogs, or intend to make speeches as the men are mowing and maids a-milking while the dew is on their eye!

But to resume.

Pharming is one of the fine arts discovered by the ancients of Ireland, under the green old sod. To be a pharmer, a man must be a pharmer whole or in part. The less he knows about it, the more he can write about it. Having a few spare moments, I bought of Carleton, the great book-maker of New York, ten copies of Greeley's "What is It?" on farming, and opened-up shop. I have read that book through nine times—twice backward, and once standing on my head! Have mastered it at last, and condense in milder shape what I know about running the thing into the ground.

Young man, be a farmer! Young woman, be a farmer! Buy a billiard-table, dust your clothes on the top of it, sprinkle on a little dandruff, and go to work. Never think of beginning with less than a field of green at least

6x10. Spread your earth all over the billiard-table evenly, to the depth of one-sixteenth of an inch, irrigate with a sponge, and subsoil to the depth of ten feet. If you have no billiard-table, buy a piece of land, if you can't get a whole one, and go to work.

The best way is to stand about in the shade, or hire out to hold a chair down in a saloon while the old man does the work.

If your farm is stony, pick out the stones before they are ripe and throw them in the road. This will cause others to McA-Dam-ize your street. Never think of ploughing less than nine feet, if your mule will pull it. If you have no team, wait till winter; then drill and blast. This will pulverize the earth, elevate your land warm it, and you will be able to report before your slow neighbors.

Run your creeks up-hill, and wash sheep only in warm water.

Pick geese on Sunday, and sit the eggs

on fence-posts, out of the way of garter-snakes.

In turning grind-stone to educate scythes, never turn the handle backward, or the early grass will wilt before the color comes to it.

Put a left-handed swivel in your scythe, so it will cut both ways.

In selecting gooseberries, pick out the crook-neck variety and put them in the nest under the best goose in the drove by the middle of October, that the goslings may be naturalized by the time for spring elections.

In harvesting strawberries, be careful not to run the thresher too fast, or the straw will be spoilt for juleps, and only fit for beds.

To cook string-beans, it is not necessary to parboil the string in more than one suds.

The best way to raise calves is to sit in a cane-seat chair and put your heels on the mantel-piece or a high table.

When washing sheep, it is best to shear them

Canary-seed should be sown in drills, so the young birds will rows early.

In planting string-beans, never use yarn—when once in the throat it is so hard to come up. The same with artichokes or pips in chickens.

Pitchforks should be sorted and packed in sugar, the juice boiled and skimmed before running into cakes.

Pumpkins should hang on the trees till frost comes; then should be picked, not shook off, and packed in sweet oil.

In stuffing sausage, do not stuff too much into your stomach, or you'll have a feline in your category, and feel that you have incurred something you hate to meat.

Dandelions should be worked in pink rather than blue worsted—they will wash better.

In putting up dried apples for market, let them lay out in the rain till the seeds start; then run them backward through a fanning-mill set to seive No. 4, with the slide well down in the hopper, while the hired girl turns the crank to the key of C-sharp.

Ordinary shoes will do for oxen when at farm-work. Use slippers on them only when going to church.

For succotash, the young corn and potatoes should be sliced and planted in the same hills the year before. Then take care not to injure the pods when the fruit is ready to tassle out.

Old rags are better than glass to stop holes in windows—the neighbors cannot see in so well.

Beach-nuts should never be eaten with their skins on—they change the complexion so.

Young bed-quilts should never be taken out of the ground in the fall, till the beds have been well spaded for the next crop.

In hatching suspenders, care must be taken that the old hen does not have her nest near the gallows, or the young birds will be hard to catch.

Look out for Protection! Let the big hogs eat the little ones, then there will be more room in the pen and less expense for barrels. But, in salting the pork, never use rock-salt on a stony farm, but feed them with fine salt from a spoon, if Butler is not in that vicinity. Use Epsom salts exclusively for horses.

Never put spots on pigs backward, except they are for army use.

Sweet corn is the best to corn beef, though old cows used to the business will eat the common red glaize, if the hired man does not yellow at them before they get into the garden.

In making pork out of pig-iron, it is not necessary to fill the tub more than half-full of lime and straw, though hickory-ashes are the best.

Use peach-leaves to color blonde, and this is all I know about farming.

Furrowily thine,

"B." P.

CHAPTER XXX.

"WHO'S BIN HERE SINCE ISH BIN GONE?"

HILLFLICKER SNICKSNACKER, a Teutonic vender of sourkraut, wooden combs, crude cabbage, striped mittens, cotton suspenders, and "liddle dings," with true patriotic zeal, left his home in La Crosse at the commencement of the war, and enlisted as a slop grocery-keeper behind the sutler's tent on the Potomac. When he went away, it was with the intention of making some "monish," if it took all summer; and nobly did he fight it out on his line. How he did it, is best told as he related it to us on his return:

"You see, Mr. Bumroy, der drum beats, und der call cooms to go to war mit arms. Ish be patriotic so much as Sheneral Washburn, or Sheneral Curtis, or Sheneral Bangs, or any tam sheneral who lifs to coom home great mans. So I puys some liddle dings, und gits some bapers from der War Committee, und goes mid der poys to be batriots, und sell some liddle dings und make some monish. I kiss mein frow five, nineteen dimes, und goes mit der war. I goes to Shambersburg und makes some monish. Vun day I pokes mein vindow out on mein head to hear der serenade, und dink of someding, ven I see dat rebel Sheneral Shtonefence Shackson, mit his droops und pig prass pand, cooming der shtreet down, playing like der tuyfel on der prass band,

"'Who's bin here since Ish bin gone?'

"Dat Shtonefence Shackson is der tuyfel mit fightins! So I puts mein monish in mein bocket, und I puts mein little bapers in mein pag, und I goes so quick as never vas to Gettysburg; und dere I opens some more liddle dings, und makes shtore mit der army. Vun day I hears sojer-droops on der horsepack riding down der shtreet like dunder, und den I pokes der vindow out on mein head und looks meinself up der shtreet, und der cooms dat tuyfel Sheneral Shtonefence Shackson, playing dat same oder dune as I hear pefore,

"'Who's bin here since Ish bin gone?'

"Den I makes mein monish coom inter mein bockets, und makes mein pag coom into mein bapers, und puts mein sign on der pig shtore on der corner, so I loses more goods as I had not got, to collect more pay from der War Committee, und den I coom to Wisconsin to see mein frow, as I don't seen in dese two years, so long time as never vas.

"Den I cooms home, und knocks on der door, und mein frow she makes talk, und tells me, 'Who's dere?'

"Den I say, 'Hillflicker Snicksnacker;' und she knows dat ish mein name, 'cos dat ish her name, too, und she make herself coom out of der house, und gif me nine, seven times kiss on mein face, so good as never vas!

"Den, Mr. Bumroy, I looks mit mine eyes, und I sees somedings! Und so I ask mein frow if she pe true to me all der time since I go off to pe a batriot? und, if she pe true to her Hill-ficker Snicksnacker, vy she make so much grow ven I pe gone two years mit der war? Und I gits mad as der tuyfel, und den I dinks of dat tam Sheneral Shtonefence Shackson und his pig brass band, und I sings,

"'Who's bin here since Ish bin gone?'

"Und now, Mr. Bumroy, somebody makes trooble mit me, for Ish bin gone two years, und I know somedings, und I goes pack mit der war, und I sings dat tam Shtonefence Shackson song all der vay,

"'Who's bin here since Ish bin gone?'"

CHAPTER XXXI.

A JERSEY ATONEMENT.

I'M like a rosebud subdrowned in honey. Yea, in a newspaper mine optics beheld lines, saying—black ink on white paper, a contrast like snowflakes on a contrabandus—that

"A RICH WIDOW OF GENTLE DISposition wants some one to love—wants to marry a congenial gentleman not over sixty, with a desire to improvement. Address, &c."

Just my age to a duck's foot! Rather ambiguous, but means well, sayeth I to I. Desire to improvement was good. Slow work for a man of sixty to greatly improve a woman, unless she be well down the steel-yard of years. I went. Quiet home—charming widow. Had seen forty winters somewhere—know not where. Handed her the paper with the delicious advertisement therein, like a raisin in a kettle of beans. She smiled over her fan. She scooched her head gently, thus. She gently bit her upper lip, and prayed—that is, prayed me to be seated. I was fresh from the districts of ruralism. I had hoed the calves, milked the bees, fed the growing potatoes, built sweet cider, and quenched my thirst with rail-fences, and was just the canary for the blooming widow's perch.

I sat in the spontaneous deliciousness of the affectionate intercourse of that enthusiastic explorer of masculine hearts five hours that night. I was like a humming-bird in a fanning-mill. I squozed the widow; the widow squizzened me. I leaned my thinking-box against her maternal instincts, and looked into her eyes as a burglar looks around a corner. And all I saw was love. Says I, "Shall we?" Says she, "Shan't we?" We went to a minister. Five dollars, and all was over.

How I revelled! Sixty years of bachelor days in New Jersey had fleetened over my head and things. I was a freshman. I was a icicle, waiting for the sun of love to thaw me out. She thawed me! We began to live. I tried to improve the widow. I spent all my evenings in improving her. She improved. We were weddened in April—April the onest. With the vigor of a Spring chronticleer did I prove my devotion. Like the first violet of vernal did I watch our &c. increase. One day, when I came home to our cot in the mill, I saw spread out on the floor a fourteen-year-old lump of ragged boy. 'Twas ragged Pete, of the Newsboy Brigade. He was on a lark. He'd been sloshing about, and had become hilarious. He showed surface indications of being drunk. I wanted to know why he camest thus upon us. He said he wanted the old woman to give him half a horse. That was Pete's idea of a $5 bill! The cherubim was the child of my adored! I gave him the lucre. He went. I wanted to caress him with the toe of my boot, but he looked too detrimental. I spoke gently to my wife about Pete. She said she meant to tell me that she had a cherub, but when she saw me, I was so enticing she forgot it! She said I made her forget it. Pretty compliment, wasn't it? I told her that her Peter mustn't be a re-peter, or I'd peter. She said five dollars a week would keep him away. I told her I was just in from the country, &c., etc.; but she did five-dollars me, and I saw no more of Peter. She said she had atoned for all that. Who could doubt her? We went on smoothly.

One day, when I came home, two half-breeds were on the family bed, playing with a shaggy-eyed dog. The half-breeds were brothers. They were twins. They were of eleven years' duration so far. They were in the boot-black business at Washington Market, and lived in a dry-goods box there. They had dark features, and a peculiar kink to their capillary. They called my consort "Mother." She had bore them. They bored me. Words failed to relieve me. I spoke of Pete. She said these were her other heavenly blessings! I asked if these had been atoned for. She said No. I felt better, for, if they had, I should have looked for four of an age, and all four clear black! I settled five dollars a week on the young Washingtons, and was again happy.

* * * * * *

This is the record of June. I've been a father for a week. Says I, Bully for New Jersey! Was married April first. Never knew an instance where improvement went on so rapidly. Age tells; blood is nothing. And such a baby! It's a pretty baby. Will be a man, if it grows up. It was like a newspaper that is well read. It has the strabismus. It has red hair. I have written to my father to know if I had red hair. Mine is like the driven over snow. Have written to my original doctor, who I used to term a cow-catcher, to know if I had the cross-eyed when first borned. Am waiting for a reply. Wife says it is because we live at the forks of the road, opposite the red barn. She may be right. I hope she is right! If I had been ninety years old, we should have had this help to our census a month ago. That is, on this principle. I have given up business. The loving disposition is proving too much for me. I sold my steers, corn-stalks, and cow-pasture. I sold them that

I might be here continually to improve the widow.

Now look at me! I'm clad in a pea-green dressing-gown. It is four o'clock in the morning. I have been walking the floor three hours. This cherub asleep in my arms is our baby. *Our first baby!* That is to say, on my part. It is our last atonement. I like baby. It's better than lobster-salad. It's a vigorous baby. It never sleeps. I feed it on paregoric, and such stimulants. I am its nurse. It eats from a bottle. I walk the floor with it. It don't seem to like me. It yells as if its father had been an auctioneer. I never auctioneered. It kicks as if its paternal derivative had at some time of life been a yackass. I never was a yackass! It squalls as if its philoprogenitor had been a storm at sea. I never was one of them. Its mother is of a loving, gentle disposition. She loves gin, and, after drinking two bottles full, or empty, becomes gentle. She is gentle now! I have tied the cherub's legs together with a piece of wire, so he can't kick; I've put a court-plaster over his mouth, so he can't squall; I've tied a strip of paling to his back, so he can't squirm; and sit down to write how this affair is culminating. I've got Pete and the two "atonements" out of the way. I've got a sure thing on the widow, while the gin holds out. And I've got a tight thing on our cherub, if the court-plaster don't burst. So now I'll let him sleep in my arms, lying like an infant on its father's lap while I write. Egad! I've got 'em all tight, and now to my letter. I feel a little dry; will take some ice-water, and go to work.

*   *   *   *   *   *

Don't answer advertisements inserted by loving widows. I have tried it, and, after a few weeks of——

Confound that young one—how it perspires! Guess I won't finish this article till I've tried on those new pants, for they may not fit, and I may have to send them back for alterations!

A Catalogue of

BOOKS

PUBLISHED BY

CARLETON & CO.,

NEW YORK.

Madison Square,

corner of

5th Avenue and Broadway.

1871.

G. W. Carleton. *G. W. Dillingham.*

"*There is a kind of physiognomy in the titles of books no less than in the faces of men, by which a skilful observer will know as well what to expect from the one as the other.*"—BUTLER.

Mary J. Holmes.

'LENA RIVERS.—	A novel.	12mo. cloth,	$1.50
DARKNESS AND DAYLIGHT.—	do.	do.	$1.50
TEMPEST AND SUNSHINE.—	do.	do.	$1.50
MARIAN GREY.—	do.	do.	$1.50
MEADOW BROOK.—	do.	do.	$1.50
ENGLISH ORPHANS.—	do.	do.	$1.50
DORA DEANE.—	do.	do.	$1.50
COUSIN MAUDE.—	do.	do.	$1.50
HOMESTEAD ON THE HILLSIDE.—	do.	do.	$1.50
HUGH WORTHINGTON.—	do.	do.	$1.50
THE CAMERON PRIDE.—	do.	do.	$1.50
ROSE MATHER.—	do.	do.	$1.50
ETHELYN'S MISTAKE.—	do.	do.	$1.50
MILLBANK.—	*Just published.*	do.	$1.50

Augusta J. Evans.

BEULAH.—	A novel.	12mo. cloth,	$1.75
MACARIA.—	do.	do.	$1.75
ST. ELMO.—	do.	do.	$2.00
VASHTI.—	do.	do.	$2.00
INEZ.—	do.	do.	$1.75

Victor Hugo.

LES MISERABLES.—	The celebrated novel,	8vo, cloth,	$2.50
DO.	Two vol. edition, fine paper,	do.	$5.00
DO.	In the Spanish language	do.	$5.00

Algernon Charles Swinburne.

LAUS VENERIS, AND OTHER POEMS.—Elegant new edition $1.50

Captain Mayne Reid.—Illustrated.

THE SCALP HUNTERS.—	Far West Series	12mo. clo.,	$1.50
THE WAR TRAIL.—	Far West Series	do.	$1.50
THE HUNTER'S FEAST.—	Far West Series	do.	$1.50
THE TIGER HUNTER.—	Far West Series	do.	$1.50
OSCEOLA, THE SEMINOLE.—	Prairie Series	do.	$1.50
THE QUADROON.—	Prairie Series	do.	$1.50
RANGERS AND REGULATORS.—	Prairie Series	do.	$1.50
THE WHITE GAUNTLET.—	Prairie Series	do.	$1.50
WILD LIFE.—	Pioneer Series	do.	$1.50
THE HEADLESS HORSEMAN.—	Pioneer Series	do.	$1.50
LOST LENORE.—	Pioneer Series	do.	$1.50
THE WOOD RANGERS.—	Pioneer Series	do.	$1.50
THE WHITE CHIEF.—	Wild Forest Series	do.	$1.50
THE WILD HUNTRESS.—	Wild Forest Series	do.	$1.50
THE MAROON.—	Wild Forest Series	do.	$1.50
THE RIFLE RANGERS.—	Wild Forest Series	do.	$1.50

Comic Books—Illustrated.

ARTEMUS WARD,	His Book.—Letters, etc.	12mo. cl.,	$1.50
DO.	His Travels—Mormons, etc.	do.	$1.50
DO.	In London.—Punch Letters.	do.	$1.50
DO.	His Panorama and Lecture.	do.	$1.50
DO.	Sandwiches for Railroad. . .		.25
JOSH BILLINGS	ON ICE, and other things.—	do.	$1.50
DO.	His Book of Proverbs, etc.	do.	$1.50
DO.	Farmer's Allmanax. . . .		.25
FANNY FERN.—	Folly as it Flies. . . .	do.	$1.50
DO.	Gingersnaps	do.	$1.50
VERDANT GREEN.—	A racy English college story.	do.	$1.50
MILES O'REILLY.—	His Book of Adventures.	do.	$1.50
ORPHEUS C. KERR.—	Kerr Papers, 4 vols. in one.	do.	$2.00
DO.	Avery Glibun. A novel. . . .		$2.00
DO.	The Cloven Foot. do.	do.	$1.50
BALLAD OF LORD BATEMAN.—	Illustrated by Cruikshank.		.25

A. S. Roe's Works.

A LONG LOOK AHEAD.—	A novel. .	12mo. cloth,	$1.50
TO LOVE AND TO BE LOVED.—	do. . .	do.	$1.50
TIME AND TIDE.—	do. . .	do.	$1.50
I'VE BEEN THINKING.—	do. . .	do.	$1.50
THE STAR AND THE CLOUD.—	do. . .	do.	$1.50
TRUE TO THE LAST.—	do. . .	do.	$1.50
HOW COULD HE HELP IT?—	do. . .	do.	$1.50
LIKE AND UNLIKE.—	do. . .	do.	$1.50
LOOKING AROUND.—	do. . .	do.	$1.50
WOMAN OUR ANGEL.—	do. . .	do.	$1.50
THE CLOUD ON THE HEART.—	do. . .	do.	$1.50
RESOLUTION.—	do. . .	do.	$1.50

Joseph Rodman Drake.

THE CULPRIT FAY.—	A faery poem, with 100 illustrations.	$2.00
DO.	Superbly bound in turkey morocco.	$5.00

"Brick" Pomeroy.

SENSE.—	An illustrated vol. of fireside musings.	12mo. cl.,	$1.50
NONSENSE.—	do. do. comic sketches.	do.	$1.50
OUR SATURDAY NIGHTS.	do. pathos and sentiment.		$1.50
BRICK DUST.—	Comic sketches.		$1.50
GOLD DUST.—	Fireside musings.		$1.50

John Esten Cooke.

FAIRFAX.—	A brilliant new novel. .	12mo. cloth,	$1.50
HILT TO HILT.—	do.	do.	$1.50
HAMMER AND RAPIER.—	do.	do.	$1.50
OUT OF THE FOAM.—	do. *Just published.*	do.	$1 50

Books of Amusement.

THE ART OF AMUSING.—With 150 illustrations. 12mo. $1.50
ROBINSON CRUSOE.—A Complete edition, illustrated, do. $1.50

By the Author of "Rutledge."

RUTLEDGE.—A deeply interesting novel. 12mo. cloth, $1 75
THE SUTHERLANDS.— do. . . do. . $1.75
FRANK WARRINGTON.— do. . . do. . $1.75
ST. PHILIP'S.— do. . . do. . $1.75
LOUIE'S LAST TERM AT ST. MARY'S.— do. . $1.75
ROUNDHEARTS AND OTHER STORIES.—For children. do. . $1.75
A ROSARY FOR LENT.—Devotional Readings. do. . $1.75

Richard B. Kimball.

WAS HE SUCCESSFUL?— A novel. . . 12mo. cloth, $1.75
UNDERCURRENTS.— do. . . do. $1.75
SAINT LEGER.— do. . . do. $1.75
ROMANCE OF STUDENT LIFE.—do. . . do. $1.75
IN THE TROPICS.— do. . . do. $1.75
HENRY POWERS, Banker. do. . . do. $1.75
TO-DAY.— do. . . do. $1.75

M. Michelet's Remarkable Works.

LOVE (L'AMOUR).—Translated from the French. 12mo. cl., $1.50
WOMAN (LA FEMME).— . do. . . do. $1.50

Ernest Renan.

THE LIFE OF JESUS.—Translated from the French. 12mo. cl.,$1.75
LIVES OF THE APOSTLES.— do. . . do. $1.75
THE LIFE OF SAINT PAUL.— do. . . do. $1.75

Popular Italian Novels.

DOCTOR ANTONIO.—A love story. By Ruffini. 12mo. cl., $1.75
BEATRICE CENCI.—By Guerrazzi, with portrait. do. $1.75

Geo. W. Carleton.

OUR ARTIST IN CUBA.—With 50 comic illustrations. . $1.50
OUR ARTIST IN PERU.— do. do. . . $1.50
OUR ARTIST IN AFRICA.—(*In press*) do. . . $1.50

Julie P. Smith.

WIDOW GOLDSMITH'S DAUGHTER.—A novel. 12mo. cloth, $1.75
CHRIS AND OTHO.— do. do. $1.75
THE WIDOWER.— do. do. $1.75

Mansfield T. Walworth.

WARWICK.—A new novel. . . 12mo. cloth, $1.75
LULU.— do. . . . do. $1.75
HOTSPUR.— do. . . . do. $1.75
STORMCLIFF.— do. . . . do. $1.75
A NEW BOOK.— do. . . . do. . $1.75

Miscellaneous Works.

FRENCH LOVE SONGS.—By the best French authors. .	$1.50
BEAUTY IS POWER.—An admirable book for ladies. .	$1.50
ITALIAN LIFE AND LEGENDS.—By Anna Cora Ritchie.	$1.50
LIFE AND DEATH.—A new American novel. .	$1.50
HOW TO MAKE MONEY; AND HOW TO KEEP IT.—Davies.	$1.50
THE CLOISTER AND THE HEARTH.—By Charles Reade.	$1.50
TALES FROM THE OPERAS.—The Plots of all the Operas.	$1.50
LOVE IN LETTERS.—An interesting and piquant book. .	$2.00
OUT IN THE WORLD.—A novel. By T. S. Arthur.	$1.50
WHAT CAME AFTERWARDS.— do. do. .	$1.50
OUR NEIGHBORS.— do. do. .	$1.50
LIGHT ON SHADOWED PATHS.—do. do. .	$1.50
ADVENTURES OF A HONEYMOON.—A love story. .	$1.50
THE BIBLE IN INDIA.—From the French of Jacolliot. .	$2.00
AMONG THE PINES.—Down South. By Edmund Kirke.	$1.50
MY SOUTHERN FRIENDS.— do. . do. .	$1.50
DOWN IN TENNESSEE.— do. . do. .	$1.50
ADRIFT IN DIXIE.— do. . do. .	$1.50
AMONG THE GUERRILLAS.— do. . do. .	$1.50
A BOOK ABOUT LAWYERS.—Bright and interesting. .	$2.00
A BOOK ABOUT DOCTORS.— do. do. .	$2.00
WOMAN, LOVE, AND MARRIAGE.—By Fred. Saunders.	$1.50
THE GAME FISH OF THE NORTH.—By R. B. Roosevelt.	$2.00
THE GAME BIRDS OF THE NORTH.— do. do. .	$2.00
PRISON LIFE OF JEFFERSON DAVIS.—By J. J. Craven.	$1.50
POEMS BY L. G. THOMAS.—	$1.50
PASTIMES WITH MY LITTLE FRIENDS.—Mrs. Bennett.	$1.50
THE GREAT TRIBULATION.—By Dr. John Cumming.	$1.50
THE GREAT PREPARATION.— do. . . do. .	$1.50
THE GREAT CONSUMMATION.— do. . . do. .	$1.50
THE SQUIBOB PAPERS.—A comic book. John Phœnix.	$1.50
COUSIN PAUL.—A new American novel. . .	$1.75
JARGAL.—A novel from the French of Victor Hugo. .	$1.75
CLAUDE GUEUX.— do. do. do. .	$1.50
LIFE OF VICTOR HUGO.— do. do. .	$2.00
THE PHILOSOPHERS OF FOUFOUVILLE.—A Satire. .	$1.50
NEGROES IN NEGROLAND.—By Hinton Rowan Helper.	$1.00
ALABAMA AND SUMTER CRUISE.—Raphael Semmes.	$1.50
CHRISTMAS HOLLY.—By Marion Harland, Illustrated.	$1.50
THE RUSSIAN BALL.—An illustrated satirical Poem. .	.25
THE SNOBLACE BALL.— do. do .	.25
THE PRINCE OF KASHNA.—Edited by R. B. Kimball.	$1.75
THE LAST WARNING CRY.—By Rev. John Cumming.	$1.50

CPSIA information can be obtained
at www.ICGtesting.com
Printed in the USA
LVHW030130210323
742063LV00002B/572

9 783382 125967